PENGUIN METRO READS

YOUR DREAMS ARE MINE NOW

Ravinder Singh is the bestselling author of *I Too Had a Love Story*, *Can Love Happen Twice?* and *Like It Happened Yesterday*. After having spent most of his life in Burla, a very small town in western Odisha, Ravinder is currently based in New Delhi. He has an MBA from the renowned Indian School of Business. His eight-year-long IT career started with Infosys and came to a happy ending at Microsoft where he worked as a senior programme manager. One fine day he had an epiphany that writing books is more interesting than writing project plans. He called it a day at work and took to full-time writing. He has also started a publishing venture called Black Ink (www.BlackInkBooks.in), to publish debut authors. Ravinder loves playing snooker in his free time. He is also crazy about Punjabi music and loves dancing to its beats.

The best way to contact Ravinder is through his official fan page on Facebook, at https://www.facebook.com/RavinderSingh.official.fanpage.

He is more frequent in his response to readers on his Twitter handle @_RavinderSingh_.

Your Dreams are Mine Now

RAVINDER SINGH

Penguin
metro reads

PENGUIN METRO READS

Published by the Penguin Group

Penguin Books India Pvt. Ltd, 7th Floor, Infinity Tower C, DLF Cyber City, Gurgaon 122 002, Haryana, India

Penguin Group (USA) Inc., 375 Hudson Street, New York, New York 10014, USA

Penguin Group (Canada), 90 Eglinton Avenue East, Suite 700, Toronto, Ontario, M4P 2Y3, Canada

Penguin Books Ltd, 80 Strand, London WC2R 0RL, England

Penguin Ireland, 25 St Stephen's Green, Dublin 2, Ireland (a division of Penguin Books Ltd)

Penguin Group (Australia), 707 Collins Street, Melbourne, Victoria 3008, Australia

Penguin Group (NZ), 67 Apollo Drive, Rosedale, Auckland 0632, New Zealand

Penguin Books (South Africa) (Pty) Ltd, Block D, Rosebank Office Park, 181 Jan Smuts Avenue, Parktown North, Johannesburg 2193, South Africa

Penguin Books Ltd, Registered Offices: 80 Strand, London WC2R 0RL, England

First published in Penguin Metro Reads by Penguin Books India 2014

Copyright © Ravinder Singh 2014

ISBN 9780143423003

Typeset in Bembo by R. Ajith Kumar, New Delhi
Printed at Thomson Press India Ltd, New Delhi

A PENGUIN RANDOM HOUSE COMPANY

To the bravehearts of this country who took a stand and refused to suffer in silence

Prologue

The Present

There was still enough time left for dusk. But the sky over the city of Delhi was getting darker with every passing minute. It was the end of May. Summer was at its peak. After breaking the previous year's record, yet again, the maximum temperature in the city was at an all-time high. To escape the hottest part of the day, in the afternoons, people preferred to stay confined to the shelter of their offices and homes. The air was dry.

But that day was very different.

That day, late in the afternoon, the sun that was usually blazing in the western sky, was untraceable. Dense dark clouds that had flown in from the east had blocked the sunlight. It never got this dark so early in the day in the capital. But that day, Mother Nature too had chosen to wear black before time—perhaps as an act of solidarity; perhaps as a mark of protest.

In no time, the sky appeared visibly angry. Sudden intermittent bright flashes of lightning tore out from behind the dark clouds. A wild sky roared in anger—loud and clear. It threatened to rain.

It certainly wasn't the arrival of monsoon. That was at least a month away. A spell of rain in the hot summer isn't uncommon in Delhi. Intense heat for a prolonged period usually led to a shower. But the manner in which the rain was preparing itself to fall over the city of Delhi that day, was not a common occurrence. It was rather scary.

A few thousand feet below the angry black clouds were many thousand angry souls who had come out on the streets of Delhi. Agitated young men and women—college students and office goers. There was rage in their eyes, their young faces, their body language. They were a mass of anger and protest. And they were loud—louder than the loudest thunderclaps. It didn't matter if they knew the person standing next to them or walking with them. They had all gathered for a cause that was common to each one of them—justice!

That was one word anyone could read on those several hundred banners and posters that the crowd unanimously brandished.

It had all become a phenomenon, which was unseen in Delhi till that evening. Every road that led to India Gate and Jantar Mantar, every train that arrived at Rajiv Chowk metro station, every bus that drove into central Delhi, was packed with youngsters. Delhi was witnessing a first of its kind mass protest. The young India that on weekends would have chosen to chill out in glamorous multiplexes to watch a movie or would have opted to sweat it out on the cricket grounds, had chosen to spend the weekend on the baked roads of Delhi.

On the other side of this young India was an old system that wasn't yet ready to change itself. It was a system that on one hand had severely failed to maintain law and order in the state, but on the other hand was trying to control the chaotic situation it was faced with. Every single policeman in the city was on alert. Clad in their khaki uniforms and protected by their helmets, the troop brandished their canes from behind the barricades.

The scene was similar at each and every epicentre of protest. The gathering at the vast space in front of Rashtrapati Bhavan was the biggest of all, seeing which the Rapid Action Force (RAF) had been installed next to the state police. From tear gas pistols to water cannons, the law and order machinery had prepared itself to deal with the situation at hand.

A gathering of thousands at this one place was a sight to behold. Every single sound, be it the frequent voices over the hundreds of walkie-talkies in the hands of cops, the centralized loudspeaker installed over the RAF's *Vajr* van, or the news journalists reporting live, all of it added to the noisy chaos. But the one sound that dominated and suppressed every other was the thumping hum of the crowd.

It remained undefeated.

Traffic that evening had come to a complete standstill. On a few key roads that led to the epicentres of the protest, the only vehicles allowed to enter were either the media vans or the police patrols. Everything else was in a deadlock.

Then came the moment when the much-anticipated occurrence happened.

It rained. Heavily.

Large drops that were powerful enough to disperse the

crowd, to make people run away from the open streets and seek the nearest shelter, fell in sheets. The scene became even bleaker. Yet it wasn't able to break the newfound will of this nation's youth standing united for a cause. *How could a spell of rain break those who'd already prepared themselves to face the monstrous water cannons?*

Besides, they were waiting for the rain anyway.

So quite miraculously, the rain only ended up uniting them. Every boy and girl, every man and woman, held each other's hands.

They made a human chain.

There was a message in it—that they were all together; that they were not going to leave and that they would brave the rain and the system.

Indeed it was an unbelievable spectacle, which looked more like a film shoot. But then our films and our society reflect each other. What often happens in society goes onto the celluloid and vice versa.

Like needles, the raindrops pierced the skin of all those present. The rain drummed over their heads. Gallons of water streamed down their faces. Eyes shrank and nostrils widened to engulf as much air as possible. Some breathed through their mouth. In no time their wet clothes clung to their wet bodies. Every gust of wind now began to appear cold.

By then, every other sound had died down. The only sound that prevailed was that of the rain. All this while the youth of Delhi stood still holding each other's hands. Many of them had been shivering. So they tightened their grip. It felt as if they were passing strength and energy to each other through their hands. It was a different Delhi that day—never heard of and certainly never seen earlier.

In that much-awaited rain of May that brought the temperature down, young India was boiling.

It was waking up from its long uninterrupted sleep.

Scores of media people and camerapersons captured it all and broadcast it live to the rest of the nation, which participated in the same emotion and aggression through this coverage.

But far away from this, where the battle between the citizens and the system was going on, there was another place—a place where a battle between life and death was in progress.

It had all begun from here—the All India Institute of Medical Sciences, well known as AIIMS.

The deathly silence in the ICU of this government hospital that evening was loud enough to wake up the entire nation. It was on every news channel. The camerapersons covered every movement of the bureaucratic and political cavalcades that arrived at the gate. The reporters captured every minute detail that the team of doctors had shared with them.

This state of affairs persisted for a long while. The world outside AIIMS continued to wait in anticipation. The sky above Delhi continued to cry.

A year ago . . .

One

That day marked the arrival of a new batch of students in Delhi University (DU). Just like the thousands of students in DU about to step into a brand new beginning, a whole new life was ready to welcome Rupali. And she was ready to embrace this life.

Rupali Sinha, an eighteen-year-old, confident, merit-list student from Patna, had made her parents proud. She had received an admission call from a top-ranked DU institute which was also her dream college. Even before she had taken her Class XII board exams, she had always dreamt of walking down the corridors of this college. She had been a bright student throughout her school life, but she knew that given the competition at the national level, it was going to be very difficult for her to make it to this institute. However, she had also believed that it was only difficult, not impossible. And with her sincerity and hard work, one day she would be there.

And so she was.

To pursue commerce from this college had been her biggest short-term goal. Except that now that she had achieved her goal, she couldn't help but feel nervous and excited at the same time. After an overnight journey and spending a good part of the day on the train, she had arrived at the college hostel in the evening. It was not too dark yet. She was soon allocated a room and given the keys and direction to the room by the warden's assistant.

It was room no. 107 on the ground floor. Rupali was relieved that she didn't have to carry her bags upstairs. She walked through the slightly dark, quiet corridor and opened the door to her room. She placed her bags on the floor and looked around the room in the faint light that entered from behind the curtains.

She smiled. It was a sweet room. Large, spacious, an iron bed each against two facing walls, two almirahs and two study tables. She had been told that she would have to share the room. But since her soon-to-be roommate hadn't arrived yet, she chose her side of the room. She then switched on the light and opened her suitcase to unpack. She took out that day's newspaper from one of her bags and laid out the sheets on the shelves of the almirah. She only arranged the few things that she would need immediately. The rest of it she planned to arrange the next evening. She slowly pulled out a bedsheet and pillowcase that her mother had so lovingly packed from the pile of clothes in her suitcase. Next came a nightie, a towel, a couple of everyday clothes, and her toiletries which she began arranging in the almirah.

Intermittently, Rupali heard voices in the corridor. She stepped out of her room to check. She saw girls who, just like her, had just moved into the hostel with their luggage. If they happened to notice Rupali, she greeted them with a smile. And they smiled back and moved on to discover their respective rooms. Rupali stepped back into her room to resume her unpacking.

She ate the leftover fruits from her journey and didn't feel hungry enough to go to the mess to eat. She left the exercise of stepping into the hostel mess to check out the place for the next day.

After arranging her room, Rupali thought about freshening up before going to bed and headed for the hostel washrooms.

As she washed her face and brushed her teeth she caught her reflection in the mirror and saw a tired-looking face with faint shadows under her eyes. She realized she had barely slept the night before leaving for the hostel. The emotional atmosphere at home and the excitement had kept her awake all night. She decided to get a good long sleep. After all, she wanted to wake up fresh for her first day at college. But when she lay on the bed, the thrill of going to college the next day kept her from dozing off. She kept tossing and turning.

When dreams take shape, sleep runs away.

The hostel bed added to Rupali's anxiety. It felt different to her body and made her uncomfortable. In that sleepless state, she began to think of home and realized how far away she was from Patna; her hostel was going to be her new home in Delhi. Minutes later, when sleep had still not come to her, she recalled all that had happened in her life in the past forty-eight hours—how her proud father, who served as a travelling ticket inspector (TTI) in North Eastern Railways, had taken a day's leave to perform a puja at home. It was to seek blessings from the Almighty, before Rupali left Patna to start college. How her caring mother, a homemaker, had made *sattu* and laddoos especially for her. As Rupali thought of her mother, she peered in the dark at the tiffin boxes which her mother had packed for her and which were now sitting on the table next to her bed. She reached out and ran her hand lovingly over them. She realized how in making them her mother had poured in all her love and care into them. She also thought of her younger brother, Tanmay, who had secretly cried all night before she was to leave for Delhi. She remembered how he had, wordlessly, given her a tight hug, probably for the first time in her life, at the Patna railway station, where her entire family had come to see her off.

This was the first time that Rupali was on her own, away from home. But she hadn't yet started missing her family or her house. There was still some time for that to happen. Instead she was happy thinking about her parents, who, unlike many other parents in Patna, or for that matter, the whole of Bihar, had given their daughter the much-needed freedom. They had allowed her to go out all by herself, to a different city, to learn how to stand on her own feet. The night passed with many such thoughts interspersed with a feeling of anticipation for what the next day would bring. It was only in the early hours of dawn that sleep finally took over her tired body.

When the morning arrived, the phone alarm broke Rupali's sleep. Through the thin curtains on the window on her right, sunlight made its way into her room. Even before she'd fully opened her eyes, Rupali slid her hand underneath the pillow and turned off the alarm. She took a moment before she got up. And when she did, she sat on her bed with her legs crossed, and folded her hands in prayer.

'Shanti! Shanti! Shanti!' she quickly whispered after which she opened her eyes again.

'Finally, the day has arrived!' she thought to herself in delight. She jumped out of bed and pulled apart the curtains. A broad smile took birth on her lips as the sun streamed through the window, flooding her room in abundant light.

The morning view outside her window was beautiful. Situated in the extreme west, her hostel offered her a view of the entire campus that spread in the east. Over the rally of trees, at a distance, she could see the giant clock on the terrace tower of the red-brick college block. And just outside her window, at the entrance of her hostel, there was a huge lawn. She could see the shrubs marking the periphery of it. In every corner of the lawn, there were more than a dozen plants with multicoloured flowers blossoming on them. Butterflies fluttered from one flower to another. A female gardener was busy watering the plants. Rupali was happy she'd got a room with a view. She loved the greenery and nature. She started humming a few lines from her favourite Hindi song as she picked up her things to go to the common bathrooms to get dressed.

'Hi! Are you from first year too?' Rupali excitedly asked the girls at the common washbasin bay, most of whom were busy brushing their teeth. Unlike the previous evening, there were many girls in the hostel that day. Some of them reciprocated Rupali's enthusiasm as they nodded vigorously with toothpaste frothing in their mouths.

Interestingly, Rupali's simple 'Hi' had broken the ice with quite a few girls who were too shy to initiate a conversation with the others till then. Soon the 'Hi' grew into a series of conversations as well as a few cross-conversations. This instantly put Rupali at the centre of every discussion that was taking place around her to the background noises of toilets flushing on the left and tap water running in the bathrooms on their right.

From introducing each other to becoming acquaintances and, from that, to discover new friends, things quickly changed into a happy chatter at various washbasins on various floors of that hostel that morning.

Unlike others, Rupali was very quick with her morning chores. She wasn't confused about what she was going to wear on her first day to college. As a matter of fact, she had already kept aside all that she was to wear—a white churidar, a pink kameez along with a white dupatta. She matched her attire with the white sandals that she had chosen for herself when her father had taken her out for shopping. She put on her pink earrings and the bangles that her brother, Tanmay, had bought for her with his pocket money. A dainty watch on her left wrist and a touch of her favourite light-pink lipstick completed her look.

Just as she was about to step out, a rhythmic tick-tack of high heels from the far end of the corridor came to a dead stop outside her room. Then there was a knock at the door.

Rupali opened the door.

There stood a girl in skin-tight blue denims and black stilettos. She was wearing a loose off-shoulder light grey T-shirt that showed off the straps of the black tank top she was wearing under it. Her sunglasses hid her eyes but exhibited her style quotient. Her jaws moved in a rhythm as she continued to chew gum.

Two

As Rupali looked on, the young girl in front of her took off her sunglasses to say 'Hi!' and introduce herself.

'I am Saloni! Saloni Chadda! If you have been allotted this room, then I am your roommate!' She raced through her sentence.

'Oh hi! I am Rupali. Come on in.' Rupali offered her hand.

Saloni happily took her hand and gave her a hug.

Rupali noticed an old man who'd come and stood behind Saloni. He gestured to Saloni who said, '*Hanji kaka, idhar andar rakh do,*' asking him to keep her luggage near the vacant bed on the other side of the room.

Rupali looked shocked. She could not help but wonder what the old man was doing inside a girls' hostel. As if reading her thoughts Saloni gave a short laugh and explained that he was her driver and had accompanied her to drop her luggage.

'Oh, that's okay,' Rupali said.

As soon as the driver left, the two of them spent a few minutes getting to know each other. Saloni told Rupali that she might not be staying back at the hostel every day since she was from Noida. And even though she didn't need to stay at the hostel, she'd chosen it to get privacy from her family.

Rupali was again shocked at what this girl told her. She would have loved it if her family lived around Delhi and if she didn't have to stay at the hostel by herself. From Saloni's clothes and behaviour Rupali could make out that she belonged to a rich family.

'She looks like a pampered child. Her father's influence must have got her this room. Otherwise in a scenario where hostel rooms are in short supply for students from other states, someone from the NCR wouldn't have managed to get one,' Rupali thought.

'Alright then, I am going to catch up with my friends in college. I will see you in the evening!' Saloni said and turned to leave.

'*Arey, arey* wait! Even I am about to leave,' Rupali said and rushed to grab her tiffin box. She picked two laddoos and offered one to Saloni.

Saloni looked at it and blew a balloon out of the gum she was chewing. When it burst in her mouth, she said, '*Muh mein chewing gum hai, agli baar kha loongi.*' (I am chewing gum. I'll take it next time.)

Rupali stood watching as Saloni left. She wondered if in the coming days the two of them would get along well with each other.

Then she looked at her watch and realized that she was getting late for the orientation programme. She placed the extra laddoo back in her tiffin box and ate the other one.

After a last-minute struggle with the door lock of her room, Rupali walked into the corridors of her hostel. As she passed by, she overheard girls in various groups chatting among themselves. She smiled at a few but didn't stop to talk with anyone. She didn't want to be late for the principal's welcome speech at the orientation venue.

With a bag hanging across her right shoulder, she walked down the paved path in between the green lawns outside her hostel. A little ahead, she passed through the line of tall ashoka trees. She looked all around her and appreciated the greenery on campus. She was happy that she had got a chance to live in such a surrounding for a few years. But as she neared the college block, with every step, her anxieties increased. It was a new beginning for her academic career.

Right in front of her stood the college in all its red-brick glory. Her eyes gleamed at the sight. She sighed. Her first day in DU had finally begun. The whole campus had been transformed into a celebration zone. It was nothing less than a festival and that too, not just for the first year students, but also for their seniors who played host to the new batch.

At the small eateries near the campus's main entrance, various students had gathered to grab a quick bite of sandwiches and other snacks. Some among them were sipping tea. Unlike the hostel, which was calm and quiet, the college block was bustling with noise. Loud conversations and laughter from various directions had given a lively energy to the campus. A majority of the hullabaloo came from the senior camps.

Amidst the crowd, the freshers could be differentiated from their seniors by their body language. The faces of the juniors radiated anxiety. It was, after all, their first day. The seniors, on the other hand, were quite confident as they looked forward to having an interesting time in welcoming the new batch and also having some fun at their cost. Only a handful of first year students seemed to be in their comfort zone, or at least they pretended to be so, because they were from Delhi. The fact that they had friends in the older batches of the same college made them feel a bit more relaxed.

An open-air amphitheatre in front of the admin block, right in the centre of the campus, was the venue for the first year students to gather. A lady who was the principal, along with a staff of a few lecturers, all men, awaited the students in the well of the amphitheatre. One of the staff members kept announcing on the mike, calling all the first year students to gather around them.

While most of the students had reached on time, a few were yet to register their attendance. Some sprinted at the last minute and joined the gathering in the semicircle, wondering if they had missed something extremely important. The principal began with a welcome note for everyone, after which she talked about the history and the greatness of the college. Giving the example of the fine alumni that the college had produced in the past, she shared her expectations of carrying on the tradition of nurturing intelligent minds and shaping them into bright individuals. A few lecturers joined her later and spoke in turns. They talked about the rules and regulations and the do's and don'ts in the campus premises. Not everything that the faculty announced made sense to the students. Half the time, the sound was the problem. Time and again the mike whistled, screeching into the ears of those standing near the speakers.

A group of super seniors who were passing by mocked the teacher on the mike by shouting, '*Sir is saal bhi aap ka mike thik nahi hua.*' (Even this year, you haven't fixed your old mike.)

Most first year students ignored it but some others made a mental note.

Taking a cue from the rules-and-regulations speech, a good number of students wanted to clarify the doubts that had cropped up in their minds after listening to the faculty. But then many of them didn't want to grab the limelight on the first day of college. So they tried to persuade their newly found friends to ask on their behalf, or thought about going to seniors to clarify these doubts for them, later in private. A few confident boys and girls did get up to ask questions on the hand mike that was passed to them, thereby registering their leadership skills among their batchmates. But most of them, in return, were offered very generic responses to their very specific questions. And that didn't leave them with a happy feeling. While, to many, the entire orientation speech appeared like a mere formality, it did fulfil one important purpose—it helped the first year students identify their batchmates.

The boys used the time to take a good look at the girls in their batch. The next thing on their mind was to learn the names of a few pretty faces who they thought they would send a friend request to on Facebook later. The girls were keener on checking each other out and knowing the latest style trends in the college.

When it came to style and fashion, clearly the Delhi girls had stolen the show. Shorts ruled. And the shorter their attire, the more attention they grabbed. With a pair of sunglasses perched on her nose, a sling bag with the strap running across her shoulder, big earrings, hair left untied and a smartphone in her hand—the typical Delhi girl was a head-turner. When it came to the boys, for a good number of them, the evergreen jeans–T-shirt or shirt remained the unofficially official attire. There were some who wore kurtas with jeans and chappals, style picked up from their seniors—that combination had become a cool fashion statement in the university.

The moment the welcome speech session was over, the new batch was asked to disperse. The students stepped out of the amphitheatre, walking towards the open lawns in the campus. And that's where their surprise of the day had been waiting for them.

Someone from the corner of the lawns had switched on the music system. A peppy number from a Bollywood blockbuster began to play. The speakers, especially installed for the day at the corners of the campus lawns, instantly came alive and caught everyone's attention. Attracted by the loud strains of foot-tapping music, students rushed towards it from every nook and corner of the college. This surprise had certainly brought a smile to every face. Gradually, the volume went up and the loud centralized woofer thumped, along with everyone's heartbeats.

All of a sudden, from somewhere in the crowd, one boy ran to the centre of the lawn and began dancing to the music. He was an excellent dancer and instantly drew a lot of attention. Heads turned and soon every eye was focused on him. The students began to clap and gather around in a circle as he continued to dance. While many from the first year didn't understand what had just happened, they surely liked what they were seeing. A smarter bunch of freshers didn't rule out the possibility that this was the first step towards the ragging that was to follow.

Some even shouted out his name. The next moment, when the track changed, a dozen boys and girls rushed to the centre of the lawn and joined him. They weren't from the batch that had assembled at the welcome speech venue. They looked like they were from a senior batch. They were all in sync and it seemed they had practised a lot before coming here.

Someone in the crowd figured it out and shouted, 'It's a flash mob!'

Then, just as suddenly, the music stopped. Everyone looked around surprised.

The euphoric crowd was about to break away when they heard a voice on the speaker.

'Hello, dear first-year students!'

Everyone began to look around to see where the voice was coming from but could not see the guy on the mike.

'We, the second year students of this college, welcome the first year students in style. Hu! Huuuuuuuuu!' he hooted.

In response, the second year batch cheered loudly.

The first year students happily continued to look here and there in search of the missing face.

The voice continued, 'So boys and girls from the first year, this flash mob is just for you. This is our first-day gift to you. So do e-n-j-o-y!' and the voice signed off in style.

At that note, the music resumed. And so did the dance. No one could find out whose voice it was.

This time all hands from the first-year batch went up. They clapped in the air, they tapped their feet on the ground. Loud screams and whistles filled the atmosphere. Undoubtedly, the ice between seniors and juniors had been broken in a brilliant way.

By the final track of the medley, the entire second year batch was performing. Surrounding them in a circle were the first year students. Ultimately, they too joined the second year batch.

When the music ended and the students paused for breath, the seniors and juniors shook hands and hugged each other. There was a cheer all around.

It had indeed been a great start to the year!

The rest of the orientation day for the freshers went in familiarizing themselves with the campus, its eateries and popular haunts. Students collected their timetables and syllabi. There was a lot of interaction with the seniors too.

After lunch there was an anti-ragging session planned by the final year students. The students' union at Delhi University had staged a street play in front of the administrative block of the college. Several members of the union had come carrying their party's official flag. Every first year student was called for the session and then there was the street play.

Not just the party in power, but other political outfits too were present at the venue. Their members wore T-shirts with their respective party's name and slogan on it. After the session was over, the volunteers of the prime opposition party in DU reached out to the first year students to sign the large white banner they had specially prepared for their anti-ragging campaign. *A ragging-free Delhi University is our vision . . .* read the white board.

As asked, the new batch pledged that they would neither tolerate ragging, and will report the matter to the administration, nor would they indulge in ragging as they moved up the academic ladder.

Amid the slogan chanting by all the parties, the second half of the day had donned a political colour. Members of all the political outfits took this as an opportunity to reach out to the new batch. They introduced themselves as well as the party's candidates who were supposed to stand for the upcoming elections. As part of their introductions, the student political outfits seized the opportunity to seek the votes and the interest of the first year students for their party.

One of the most awaited days for Rupali had turned out to be a very eventful one. But it was coming to an end. She had thoroughly enjoyed her first day on campus. In the evening, when the girls from her batch were busy talking to their new friends, Rupali was out alone on the lawn in front of her hostel, the one that was visible from the window of her room.

In one of the corners, close to the road, she had dug out some earth. Her hands were soiled and dirt clung to the ankles of her churidar. Away from the hostel that by evening had turned vociferous, the atmosphere in the garden area in front of the girls' hostel was peaceful. Hardly anyone walked in and out of the hostel at that time of the day. As Rupali continued to dig out the earth, she kept humming a song.

She was completely involved in her chore when all of a sudden, a racing jeep braked and abruptly came to a halt on the road, right in front of Rupali. The sound of the vehicle coming to rest at once broke Rupali's concentration. She looked up, surprised.

It was an open green jeep with banners stuck on both

sides of the vehicle. A few party flags were lying on the back
seat of the jeep where two boys sat facing each other. There
was another boy seated next to the guy at the wheel. All four
of them were wearing kurtas and jeans and looked like they
were seniors who certainly belonged to some political party.

As soon as Rupali spotted them, she quickly picked up
her dupatta that was lying next to her on the ground and
draped it back on. The sudden arrival of senior boys made
her extremely conscious. Both the guys on the front seat got
out of the vehicle and walked towards her. A hesitant Rupali
got up and went back a step or two.

'*Yeh gaddha kyun khod rahin hain aap?*' (Why are you
digging this hole?) asked the guy who had been driving the
vehicle. The thick beard on his face and his deep voice scared
Rupali. Her heart raced.

'Ahm . . . actually, I was . . .' Rupali had only managed to
say that, when she was suddenly interrupted.

'*Jab Hindi bhaasha mein sawaal kiya hai maine, to kya aap
Hindi mein uska uttar nahi de saktin?*' (When I have asked you
the question in Hindi, can you not respond in Hindi?) the
guy with the beard interrogated her. '*Kahaan ki rahne wali
hain aap?*' (Which place are you from?) he asked another
question.

'*Ji hum Patna, Bihar ke rahne waley hain,*' (I am from Patna,
Bihar) she replied hesitantly.

'*Hum?*' the guy on the front seat picked up on her
response, looked at his friends and burst into laughter. They
too laughed.

The guy with the beard kept staring at Rupali and only
passed a smile that wasn't as offensive as the laugh.

'Are you just one or are you too many?' the bearded guy asked her, this time in English. Rupali was surprised at his sudden switch of language. He was flawless in both.

Rupali couldn't say anything, but kept wondering for a while. Even though she gathered enough courage to speak up, she stammered, 'Sh . . . Shall I . . . a . . . a . . . answer in English or . . . in . . . in Hindi?'

This led to another bout of laughter amongst the gang. The bearded guy didn't even smile, but a moment later, he said, 'You don't need to answer that one.'

Rupali sighed with relief and wiped the sweat on her forehead. And while doing so, she unknowingly ended up smearing the dirt from her hands on her forehead.

'So tell us, why were you digging?' the guy resumed the conversation and folded his arms across his chest.

In response, Rupali bent down and picked up a small plastic bag to her left. She opened it in front of everyone and pulled out a sapling from within it. She showed it to everyone.

It was a tiny tulsi plant.

'I was about to plant this,' she said without fumbling this time.

'Lo bhai, to ab Patna, Bihar waley, Delhi mein harit-kranti le ke aayenge!' (So, now the people from Patna, Bihar, will bring the green revolution to Delhi!) one of the two boys on the back seat of the jeep said sarcastically and clapped his hands. His friends joined in.

Suddenly, the bearded guy raised his hand, gesturing at them to stop.

'Don't we have enough plants already in the campus and hostel?' he asked Rupali.

'No, it's not like that,' she said in haste.

'Then what's the need for this one?' the front-seat guy probed.

All this while, a miserable Rupali kept wondering if she could ask them who they were and why they were asking her so many questions. But then something told her not to.

Unable to hold eye contact for too long with the older boys, whom she didn't even know, Rupali first framed her thoughts and then answered softly, 'Today is my first day in this campus. It will be the first day for this plant in this campus as well.' She wondered if her answer was making any sense to them.

However, she continued, '. . . For the next few years, as I grow here, I also want to see this plant growing along with me. This plant is the symbol of my dreams. I want to take care of it. One day, I will leave this campus, but this plant will continue to be here. Even when I am gone.'

For a while she didn't hear any counter-questions to her response. So she raised her eyes to look up at the face of the guy who stood in front of her. He was staring at her with his deep dark eyes. He didn't say anything. The rest of the boys looked at each other and waited for their leader to interrogate her further. But he didn't say a single thing. He simply walked back and sat behind the wheel again. Unable to understand his state of mind, the other guy too walked back and sat inside the jeep.

The ignition was turned on. The accelerator pressed. And in no time, the jeep left. Amid the leftover smoke from the exhaust of the jeep, a relieved yet anxious Rupali stood there with the sapling in her hand. Her eyes followed the jeep till it took a turn behind the hostel block.

By then she'd forgotten the song she had been singing.

Three

The semester had finally begun. The festivities were over and a serious academic life had made its way into the lives of the hundreds of students. No one realized how quickly the first week of college got over. After a busy week filled with classes and taking notes, the first weekend offered a much-needed break to the students to adjust to their new lives.

Besides completing their college assignments, the students utilized the weekend to finish pending tasks like buying new prepaid SIM cards, updating phonebooks and so on. Some first year students shuffled their rooms in the hostel based on new friendship circles that had sprung up at the college canteen and in the corridors of the hostels. The newly formed groups of girls also went out to watch a recently released movie. While a majority of the boys stayed back to play a game of cricket within their hostel compound, some went out to explore the option of buying a second hand bike for themselves.

Within a week of the first semester, friendships and acquaintances, from the real world had also got transferred to the online world. Friend requests, in bulk, had been sent and accepted on Facebook. In some interesting cases, the smart girls had made the desperate boys wait for too long, only to reject their friend requests later. Who was single and who was in a relationship, was all clear by the end of the week.

But unlike others, Rupali wasn't a social-networking buff at all. She didn't even have a Facebook account. Saloni, her roommate, had found this very odd. She could not imagine a life that was only led in the real world. She insisted that Rupali open an account. But Rupali stuck on in her refusal. And when Saloni failed to persuade Rupali with her reasoning, she made a funny move to convince her. She made Rupali swear on her brother Tanmay's photograph that adorned Rupali's study table.

Rupali was truly shocked. *Why was it so important to have an FB account*? And why was Saloni so dramatic always?

Seeing her roommate's astonished face, Saloni immediately thought of another argument. Certainly, she wasn't going to give up so soon.

'*Arey baba,* you will be able to connect with Tanmay so easily on Facebook. Don't you want your family to see your pictures from your hostel life?'

Now that was a master stroke! *Why hadn't she thought of it before!* Of course Rupali wanted her family to see her in her new set-up, but she still wasn't sure.

But that was enough for Saloni. She had her foot in the door. And within an hour, she had finally taken her roommate to the digital world. Rupali had a Facebook profile along with a profile picture freshly clicked on Saloni's 6-megapixel phone—something that helped Saloni justify the need as well as the price tag of her beloved gadget.

Interestingly, unlike Saloni's previous claim that she would not stay back in the hostel on weekends, she did stay that whole weekend. Rupali wondered if her roommate would ever think of leaving the hostel and going back to her parents' place.

~

It was the middle of the second week. After the classes had gotten over, Rupali as usual was on her way back to her hostel when her eyes fell on the notice board. A florescent A4-size paper with pictures of musical instruments on its margins hung from the top of the board. The pictures on that bright page caught her attention. She stopped in order to take a closer look. As she read, a big smile appeared on her face. It was an invitation. The official music club of the college had invited the first-year batch to join them. It talked about a selection process that had a round of auditions, which were due late that afternoon.

Rupali loved singing. In Patna, she had been an active member of her school's music club. Having won a couple of prizes and lots of accolades in her school, she had always dreamt of participating in one of the music reality shows. Had it not been for the limited memory of her mobile phone, she wouldn't have had to delete old songs to accommodate new ones. Downloading songs to her phone and managing the limited memory of her mobile had become her biweekly routine. She had planned that the day she would earn her own money she would buy a good multi-gig song storage device for herself. Not just that, she had plans to buy and instal a

Dolby surround sound system in her house, that she would switch on every morning while she got ready for work. Music kept her going. Even when she was alone in her room or busy doing something on her own, she would keep humming her favourite songs. A habit which her friends and family found annoying at times because she completely lost herself in the songs and refused to even hear them. So when she saw the notice for the music club, she didn't need to think twice about appearing for the auditions. On her way back to her hostel, she kept thinking of the song she would sing.

In the excitement of joining a music club, she could not eat her meal properly. And once she'd decided on the song, she rehearsed it a few times in her room. It was one of her favourite ghazals from an old Hindi movie named *Bazaar*. Sung by the legendary Lata Mangeshkar, the ghazal had peculiar lyrics—*Dikhaai diye yu, ke bekhud kiya*— something that made it very special for her. She remembered the lyrics by heart. Her attempt at practising it in her room had partly woken up Saloni, who was in the habit of taking an afternoon nap because she stayed up partying till late in the night.

When Rupali was about to step out of her room, Saloni asked her what was she up to.

On finding out the reason she giggled in her lightheadedness and said, 'Is that the reason you have been humming for so long?'

'Yeah,' Rupali responded, a little embarrassed.

'Who is going with you for the audition?' Saloni asked turning on her side to make herself more comfortable.

'I don't know about the others. I read the invite on the

college notice board and made up my mind to go for it. All right, I am leaving now!' she said and stepped out of the room.

'Okay, good luck!' Saloni shouted behind her and went back to sleep.

Rupali reached the audition venue. It was to be held in a classroom on the second floor. As the classes were over for the day, the whole building seemed way quieter than in the mornings. However, there were a few students busy installing the acoustics and instruments.

Rupali looked from one side of the spacious room to the other. The benches in the front rows near the blackboard had been pushed to the sides. A guy who was trying to unwind the tangled wires of a few electric guitars noticed her and asked, 'Yes?'

'I am here for the audition,' she said enthusiastically.

The guy looked at his wristwatch and said, 'Then you are well before time for that. There are fifteen more minutes to go.'

'Oh!' she uttered, a little too loudly.

Suddenly everyone looked up from what they were doing and stared at her.

She smiled nervously, unsure of what to do with herself. She looked at her watch. In her excitement she had not paid attention to the time. She began to wonder if she should wait there or come back later as she didn't know anyone there.

'Don't worry, till the time we start, you can wait here,' a girl suggested. She seemed to be the only other female in that classroom apart from Rupali.

Rupali felt comfortable with that. 'Okay, thanks,' she said with a smile.

The girl walked towards her and asked, 'So you are from the first year, right?'

'Yes. My name is Rupali. Back at my school, I used to sing. I am so happy to see a music club here in college. When I read about today's audition I got very excited. That's the reason I came early . . .' Rupali blurted.

The other girl smiled. 'Nice to meet you. I'm Sheetal from the final year and this is our band. Let me introduce our band to you. That's Swami,' she said pointing towards a thin guy with a longish beard. 'He plays the drums as well as the tabla. Raghu and Mirza over there play the electric guitar. And that is Harpreet,' she said introducing a tall guy with a turban and clear fair skin. 'He plays the keyboards. Tenzing is a vocalist and our lead singer. He represents our club at the university level. The DU crowd loves him when he sings . . .'

As she continued to take a few more names, the members responded by either waving a hand or by smiling back. Tenzing seemed to have the most playful carefree smile, Rupali noted.

'We all are from different streams and different years and we look forward to welcoming a few students from your batch into our club too,' Tenzing shouted while bringing the mike up to his level.

Rupali smiled. She would love to be a part of this group, she thought.

By the time the instruments were fully installed, it was already ten minutes past four. A little over the time they had been asked to report. By then all the music enthusiasts from Rupali's batch had gathered in the room. Rupali counted that there were some seven of them, apart from her. She was the only girl.

The club had planned to start the audition process with their self-introductions by playing a number. It was a musical introduction-cum-welcome from the club members for the new students keen on joining.

The band tuned their guitars and synced them with the keyboard and the guy on the tabla tuned his instruments at the right scale.

'Ready?' Tenzing asked aloud. Everyone nodded.

'1 . . . 2 . . . 3 . . . 4 . . .' and fingers ran on the strings of the guitar and tapped over the tabla. All of a sudden the classroom came alive with the vibrations and the melody of the instruments. Within seconds the pulsating tune energized everyone present, especially the newcomers who began tapping their hands and feet to the rhythm. It was a piece by a Pakistani Sufi band.

Rupali was delighted and one could see it on her glowing face. She knew the lyrics well and couldn't wait for the singer to pick up the first line. And when he did, she sang along. The members of the music club, who were not participating, boosted the morale of their friends by cheering in bursts throughout the performance.

After five minutes or so, when the song ended, everyone gave the band a thundering applause. The performance, on the one hand, had set high expectations for those who had gathered to give the audition, and on the other hand, had charged up everyone to give their best.

When the audition began, Rupali was the first to sing. Two

of the boys from the first year, who were there to play the instruments, too joined her. One occupied the seat behind the congo and another stood behind the keyboards.

They took a few minutes to discuss how to go about it. The guy on the keyboards wasn't too sure if he knew the scale and the tune of this ghazal from a much older decade. But he said that he would try to manage. As soon as they were ready, the keyboards guy gave a thumbs up. Rupali nodded and closed her eyes. She was about to start.

Rupali began with a long *aalaap*, which was her own customized addition to the ghazal. But before she could arrive at her first pause to catch a breath, something happened. She heard a loud noise approaching the room. She opened her eyes in fear. Everyone was looking towards the door. Suddenly, a mob of about a dozen people rushed in and began vandalizing the whole set-up.

'You will now sing in classrooms . . . *haan*? What is this—a classroom or your music school . . . haan?' Someone in the approaching mob shouted.

'Break their fucking guitars and their bloody mikes,' someone else yelled.

'This must be this chinki's idea to do events in classrooms now,' someone else passed a racial comment on Tenzing.

Tenzing wanted to react. He was in two minds. As the mob outnumbered their gathering he didn't have much of a choice. Besides, there were two girls with them. His first priority was to safeguard the students and then his instruments. It wasn't wise on his part to get into a scuffle.

The suddenness with which all that happened didn't give

him enough time to make up his mind. The next second, there were noises of benches being thrown here and there and of people breaking the instruments.

The first year students who had come for the audition stood up in shock. The guys from the music group jumped to stop a few in the mob. They shouted their names and asked them what they were upto. Sheetal ran towards Rupali to protect her. She pulled her against the wall, next to the blackboard. Tenzing and his team attempted to save their instruments. They kept shouting at a few people in the group, asking them to stop the ruckus. But the mob outnumbered the members of the group. Luckily, no one hit anyone.

Before anyone could make any sense of what was happening, a guitar was broken, the drums were punctured and a raw fear was instilled in the minds of the newcomers.

Four

'But who were these people?'

Later in the evening that day, at Shafi's teashop, members of the music club, along with the first-year students, had gathered.

Behind a wide serving area at the counter sat Shafi, the owner, who was known for his jolly nature. It wasn't just a teashop. For anything, the painted red sections on the otherwise white walls of the shop advertised the branding of Coca-Cola. Stacks of crates with empty cold drink bottles along with two fridges full of sealed bottles stood next to each other just outside the shop. The shop served all sorts of packaged snacks and offered a limited variety of evening snacks like samosas and pakodas. Yet, the shop was called a teashop, for the special masala tea it served. Even students from other colleges which were not in the immediate vicinity of the shop would turn up at Shafi's to sip a cup of this speciality. Shafi took great pride in telling the world that he used some unique herbs in his tea. When his customers enquired about the same, he would take similar pride in telling them that it was his trade secret. Not that he hadn't ever revealed it to anyone. Till not so long back he used to do so. But he stopped telling people the day he learnt that even the makers of Coca-Cola that he sold, did not share their trade secret.

People humoured Shafi's pride in his concoction for the good-natured guy that he was. They didn't bother him much as long as they were assured that he wasn't using any drug in his tea. To add to the aesthetics of Shafi's teashop was a huge banyan tree rooted only a few feet away from his shop, with its magnificent branches spreading out in various directions over his shop. Shafi had intelligently placed two dozen fibre chairs and a couple of tables under the shade of that banyan, thereby making it a perfect hangout for students.

The meeting that evening at Shafi's teashop wasn't planned. It was Tenzing's idea to bring everyone there. He wanted to use the opportunity to talk to everyone and calm them down.

Apart from being the leading member of the music club at college, Tenzing was also the head of the cultural club at the university. He felt it was his responsibility to clarify the matter.

'Please listen to me guys,' he said addressing the group.

Tenzing updated the first year students that a year before, their music club had performed in an event organized by the present party in power in the students' union. Back then, that party was not in power. The music club was not aware that the leaders of that party wanted to gather the crowd through a music event and later make their appeal for vote to them. The club was never into any election gimmick and had always stayed away from political equations. But the party had managed to keep them in the dark till the very end of the show. They were told that the event was meant to raise a voice in favour of improving student life on campus. It was about implementing new ideas that the students wanted to introduce and to do away with the administration's outdated policies. In all, it was an event meant to make some noise in the deaf ears of university administration. Tenzing and his team were promised that it wouldn't be political activity in any way. But once they had performed and the crowd cheered for them and against the DU authorities, the present leading party broke its promise. They announced that the band favoured their party and appealed to the crowd to vote for them. The very next day the music club had officially denied the allegations of supporting their political party, or for that matter supporting any party in DU. But the damage was already done. In the next few weeks, the party played various populist games and came to power after the elections were held.

Unfortunately, the party that got voted out never believed their clarifications. Their members continued to think that the music club was the prime cause for their defeat, or at least, that it all started from the show it had performed. The impact of their performance on the elections was high because of the clean image of the members of the music club and the issues which they had stood for in the past.

'The guys who vandalized the set-up today, are people from that very party that was voted out,' Tenzing said.

As he finished, Tenzing kept the empty glass of tea back on the table. He looked at the faces around him. Everyone was listening to his story with keen interest. For the present members of the club, it was an unpleasant walk down memory lane. Something they wished they could undo.

'So does that give them the right to vandalize things whenever they want? Can't we complain against them?' the guy who was supposed to play the congo asked.

Tenzing looked at him and thought for a second before he spoke again. 'We can. But this time we had unintentionally provided them the opportunity to do so.'

No one understood what Tenzing meant when he said that. So he clarified, 'Actually, we have a dedicated music room. And we are supposed to practise in that room only. To perform anywhere on campus we need to take official permission, something that we didn't do this time. The voltage has been fluctuating in the music room for the past few weeks. Two of our electronic guitars have gone bad and the adapter of the keyboards is dead because of this fluctuation. The administration was supposed to fix the issue but as usual the music room isn't their priority. Taking permission to practise in a different place is a long process and the department generally doesn't allow this. Else, we would have this audition in the first week of the new session itself.'

'But then we had also assumed that the department would fix the electrical mess in the music room, which they didn't till the last day, despite our requests. With no choice left, we thought of using one of the classroom after college hours. Moreover, the party members who destroyed our set-up today had been lying low for a long time. So we thought we could go ahead without fear.'

Tenzing paused for a moment and continued '... that plan now has gone for a toss. Those guys must have somehow found out that we hadn't taken permission.' As he sighed at their lapse in judgement he felt a hand on his shoulder.

'*Chal koi na yaar!* Never mind. These things happen.' It was Sheetal patting his shoulder, trying to cheer him up.

A moment of silence passed. People took their time to digest the logic behind what had happened. It still appeared illogical that anyone could come and damage things just like that. Some of them sipped the tea slowly, thinking about it all. Some of them hung their heads in disappointment. Some played with the empty tea glasses between their hands on the table and kept staring at them.

'So what do we do now? Can't we take the help of the party that is at present in power? After all, even though it was unintentional from the music club's side, the club is an important reason behind their coming to power. They will surely help us.' This was Rupali who'd thought a lot about this.

'That's not an option for us. As a cultural club we have clearly protested against the ruling party's actions last year. If we reach out to them, it will only justify what they had been claiming till now—that we sang for them. We don't want to make this political again,' Sheetal said.

Tenzing then got up and announced, 'We will meet after a week. Meanwhile, I will seek permission from the administration to issue us a specific place to practise.'

'Alright, then! Now let's change the topic and talk about something else,' Sheetal offered and a few people smiled.

'I agree, how about another round of tea, guys?' Tenzing raised his empty glass.

'*Kya baat hai, Tenzing!* Another round of tea for the juniors!' Harpreet teased him.

'And Shafi bhai, samosas only for Harpreet!' Tenzing shouted, looking towards the teashop counter.

Harpreet looked confused, wondering why Tenzing was being so nice to him.

'You are going to repair the broken instruments, na!' Tenzing chuckled.

Everyone laughed as Harpreet made a face.

With that everyone began chatting amongst themselves. While the juniors talked about their personal backgrounds, the members of the music club shared their insights from their college and campus so far. They told stories about a few interesting musical nights that they had hosted in the past and the awards that they had bagged in inter-college competitions.

Sheetal mentioned a few funny events from her memory of previous year's annual festival at the university level. With great joy Harpreet narrated how Tenzing was in the middle of singing a patriotic song when he received an electric shock from his mike on stage. Instantly, he ended up saying 'O *Bhen★★★★*' on his mike. Everyone heard him and the whole patriotic mood went for a toss. The crowd whistled and shouted—'Once more! Once more!'

Listening to that, laughter erupted all around the tables outside Shafi's teashop. It lightened the mood. Rupali felt a bit awkward at that, but Sheetal's joyful presence next to her helped. Soon the samosas arrived, not just for Harpreet, but for everyone.

That evening the group didn't play any music, but a new bond developed on the grounds of a common interest— music. The auditions appeared to be a mere formality now. Rupali would be in the group for sure. As the only girl who had appeared for the audition, she turned out to be the right replacement for Sheetal, who was going to pass out of DU the same year.

But amidst all this, Rupali was thinking about something

else; rather someone else. It was a face that had looked familiar. The face she had seen among those who had gatecrashed and disrupted the auditions. He hadn't stepped inside the class, but had stood at the entrance, his arms folded across his chest, just like the other day. Just when they were all stepping out of the vandalized classroom, she had tried to recall that face. And when she succeeded in doing so, it came as a shock—he was the same guy who had interrogated her on the evening when she had been planting the sapling.

Five

'What are you saying?' Rupali asked Saloni in sheer disbelief.

It was late in the night and as usual the two roommates were busy gossiping. Their chat sessions had started almost a month ago and, while Saloni would often transform their midnight talk into bitching sessions, Rupali would sit listening carefully. Most times, Rupali wasn't too bothered about what she heard but she enjoyed being with Saloni and having a friend to talk to. For Saloni there was the satisfaction of talking her heart out and sharing what was on her mind with someone who she knew to be a sensible girl—the kind didn't exist in her own social group.

But it wasn't that Saloni thought of Rupali as only a good friend and a mature girl whom she could trust. There had been times when Saloni had also helped Rupali.

Improving Rupali's style quotient and making her more fashionable was always on Saloni's to-do list.

'I swear to change your typical *behenji*-type fashion sense into a cosmopolitan one. And if I do not, you can change my name,' Saloni had claimed and she made sure she stuck to her words. There was rarely a day on which she did not advise

Rupali on what to take off and what to try on. Saloni, who was usually possessive about all her belongings, was generous with Rupali. She would often encourage her friend to wear her accessories, in spite of several refusals from Rupali. As much as Rupali appreciated her roommate's gesture, she was embarrassed on certain occasions, especially when Saloni would change her clothes in front of her. Rupali would turn her head to give Saloni the privacy that she never asked for. Saloni was a confident and bold girl who did not have any problems in undressing in front of her roommate. On one occasion, when, after taking a bath, Saloni entered the room and threw aside her wet towel, she had especially asked for her roommate's attention.

'See, I bought this polka-dotted bra for myself. Isn't it sexy?' she had said while trying to hook it on.

Rupali had to battle her sense of shame to look at her roommate's bra and appreciate it. But gradually, she learnt to adjust to hostel life.

At times, Rupali found it extremely difficult to accept Saloni's idea of westernizing someone who had lived all her life in the desi attire of salwar kameez. Not that she had anything against western clothes like jeans and skirts, but she felt uncomfortable in these clothes. Though, she had to admit to herself, sometimes she wished to try them on. However, she would also wonder about what her parents would think if they saw her in short skirts. Rupali's battle between her wishes and fears was an interesting and challenging space for Saloni to invade and influence.

But come midnight and Saloni wasn't her style coach any more. Instead, she expected her friend to react to her anecdotes from the day.

'Really? You brought him here?' Rupali exclaimed, double-checking if what she had heard moments before was correct.

'Shhhhh!' Saloni hushed, placing her finger on her lips, her eyes wide open. Then she looked at the door in order to make sure that it was locked from inside.

Rupali tried to control her reaction. She asked again, but this time in a soft yet suspicious voice. 'You brought Imran here, to THIS room?'

Saloni nodded, her eyes gleaming with mischief as she smiled proudly, almost as if she was expecting a pat on her back from her roommate for her bravery. After all, she had sneaked in a boy to the girls' hostel, that too in broad daylight!

Rupali held her head in dismay. She immediately looked around her, wondering what all Imran would have seen in the room that was personal to her.

'How come you . . .' Rupali hadn't even completed her protest, when Saloni cut her off midway and said, 'Don't worry, as usual your portion of the room was neat and tidy and nothing was out. So Imran didn't see anything. In any case he was more interested in me than in your stuff. Okay?'

Rupali wasn't convinced. She looked worried.

'*Teri itni phatt ti kyun hai yaar?*' (Why do you get so scared?) Saloni tried to comfort her in her own way.

Rupali didn't know what to say. She was just not comfortable with having a boy in her room, that's it. *Why could Saloni not understand that!*

'Hello! Madam! I am having an affair. Not you! So don't be worried about anything. Chill!' In her excitement Saloni got up from her chair and shifted onto her bed. She sat cross-legged. She was overjoyed to reveal all that had happened after she'd secretly sneaked Imran into their room. She had expected Rupali to say, 'Oh my God! Really? How did you do that? Teach me also, na!' But all she got was silence.

Rupali lay on her bed staring at Saloni. She wondered if her roomie was gutsy or mad. She decided Saloni was a bit of both.

'You are unbelievable!' Rupali finally spoke, shaking her head. In spite of herself, she could not hold back her smile.

Saloni took that gesture as her reward for her brave act. She threw her hands up in the air and smiled back. Then she blew a few flying kisses.

'You're mad!' Rupali laughed and further asked, 'But isn't Imran from science section?'

Seeing her roomie's level of interest increase, Saloni replied, 'Yes, he is! But how did you know?'

'I just know. But you first tell me, how did you guys meet?' Rupali inquired.

An overexcited Saloni jumped out of her bed and jumped in to join Rupali on her bed.

'Udhar ho, phir sunaati hun saari kahaani.' (Make some space, and I will tell you the whole story.)

Saloni loved telling stories. She also knew how to make them spicy and extra gossipy. She derived a lot of pleasure in narrating the whole episode of how she had met Imran, for the very first time, at the basketball court. It had happened in the first week of the semester. It wasn't love at first sight for her. But she had definitely found Imran to be one of the most handsome guys in the first year batch.

While she was an amateur in the game of basketball, Imran was a champion. Besides his good looks, Imran's sporty personality was like icing on the cake. Saloni herself was a head-turner on campus. They'd met quite by coincidence.

There weren't many girls who played basketball in the first year. One late evening, Saloni had jogged to the basketball court. But finding no one there she decided to jog back to the hostel. Suddenly, she heard someone shout, asking her to stop.

Saloni turned around to see Imran. He stood on the other side of the court in the dark, holding the ball in his hands. It took Saloni a few seconds to spot him in the darkness. Imran switched on the floodlights from the corner of the court. The lights took their time to come on, only gradually lighting up the court.

'You came here to play?' Imran asked as he walked towards Saloni, juggling the ball in his hands.

'Yes, but the other girls haven't come today. I am not sure why,' Saloni said.

'That's strange, not many boys turned up today as well and, those who did, left early. That's why I had just switched off the lights,' Imran explained.

Then there was silence as both didn't have anything to say. They looked at each other and smiled. The two of them knew each other's names, but they pretended as if they didn't. So they introduced themselves. Then Imran offered his hand for a handshake. Saloni was delighted to accept. Secretly, Imran was overjoyed feeling Saloni's palm in his own hand.

They might not have officially known each other, but they had definitely had a few quick interactions on the court earlier—sometimes while passing the ball, it fell into the other side of the court. But that evening was definitely the first time when they were alone together, with no one else around them. The darkness around them till the floodlights came on actually helped to build a bond. Till then, they had been mere acquaintances. But after that evening, their lives took a different turn. Imran invited Saloni to play a game, if she didn't mind—just the two of them.

'I . . . I don't know. I am not very good at the game . . . And we don't even have the team,' she blurted out. Of course she wanted to play with Imran when no one was there. *Then why had she given this silly excuse?*

She didn't know. She only cursed herself and wished if by some means she could take her words back.

Imran came to her rescue and offered a quick reason for Saloni to play. 'Oh! We can just play a half court three-pointer. And don't worry, I'll help you,' he said with a smile.

Saloni nodded. She was looking forward to Imran's company. They played for about half an hour, enjoying each other's company.

Saloni gave Rupali, who listened in rapt silence, a detailed description of how wonderful it had been.

'Oh baby, you should look at him when he jumps to dunk the ball. He holds the ring and does a chin-up. Too hot to handle!' Saloni said clapping her hands, her eyes twinkling as she recounted her love story so far.

Rupali heard her as if it was a magical story. *Was she going to have her own love story? Would anyone ever fall in love with her?*

Six

One hot afternoon, Rupali stepped out of her hostel for a brief interaction with one of her professors to clear a doubt she had regarding his paper. Prof. Mahajan taught accounts in the college. He was one of the more well-known faculty members. Getting a 10-minute one-to-one meeting with him was a big deal and he had accepted Rupali's request only after seeing her enthusiasm on the subject. 'If I am here day after tomorrow, you can come by 2 p.m.,' he had said.

Rupali wouldn't have required to meet Prof. Mahajan in person had it not been for the upcoming student union elections that had disrupted classes in the entire DU in an unimaginable way. Prominent walls of the campus buildings shamelessly mocked the election regulators' norm of not pasting bills and posters on the wall. They were all over the place, from the main entrance gates to inside the college toilets.

Amid the high drama of political outfits announcing their manifestos and their candidates, the loud sloganeering and clashes in the campus, and the numerous print media reporters hovering around, attending classes was the last thing on students' minds.

But then there were students like Rupali, who instead of wasting their time, thought of utilizing the same to kick-start their upcoming project work for the semester. Politics never interested Rupali. She was far apart from the world of elections, so much so that, unlike the majority of DU students, she didn't even know who all were standing for the posts and which parties they belonged to. She wasn't too sure if she knew the names of all the political outfits fighting the elections in DU and it didn't bother her. She had her priorities. She had come all the way from Patna to Delhi to study. She wanted to stay away from taking sides in campus politics.

Rupali and Saloni were in the same project group. Both of them had one individual project, as well as one group project to complete by the subsequent month-end. When it came to her group project, Rupali had little expectation from Saloni. In fact, Saloni had opted to do a project with Rupali because she knew that she could relax and let the studious girl in their group complete it. Any interference from her would only bring the quality down, is what she kept reminding Rupali.

Given the circumstances in college and the nature of her roommate, Rupali thought it wise to use the election period to accomplish as much of the project as possible. The project was on the subject of accounts and she sought Prof. Mahajan's time with regard to the same.

Rupali reached the college on time. The unofficial mass bunk of all classes had turned the college block into a lifeless building. The open lawns and the main administrative blocks stole the limelight—for they were the new centres of mass gatherings.

She walked into the college building amid the abandoned classrooms and took the staircase to go straight to the accounts department.

But when she reached Prof. Mahajan's cabin, she found the door locked. She looked at her watch. It was exactly 2 p.m. She wondered if she should hang around for a while. The professor could have been held up.

When he did not arrive even after ten minutes of her waiting, she went to look at other faculty members' cabins in the department to check if, by any chance, Prof. Mahajan was there. She checked the HOD's office as well. But to her dismay, she didn't find anyone from the department. In fact, she didn't come across a single human in the area. The whole floor was desolate!

Rupali was about to walk back in disappointment when, all of a sudden, she heard someone running up the staircase in her direction.

It turned out to be the peon who worked in the accounts department.

Finally seeing a face on that deserted floor, Rupali quickly asked him, *'Bhaiya, Prof. Mahajan kahan hai, pata hai?'* (Do you know where Prof. Mahajan is?)

'Prof. Mahajan! Hmmm . . .' the peon murmured as he looked up at the ceiling, trying to recall where he had last seen the professor.

She kept waiting till the peon looked back at her, only to shake his head from left to right.

No, he hadn't seen him around. So he turned back to leave.

Giving out a sigh of disappointment, Rupali placed her notebook back in her bag. She had no choice but to go back to her hostel. Suddenly, her phone rang. The sound of the phone shocked her as it echoed in the empty corridor. She quickly pulled it out of her bag and looked at the number. It was her brother Tanmay calling from Patna. This sort of cheered her up. She quickly zipped her bag and picked up the call.

'Hello,' she said smiling.

'HELLO!' she said loudly the second time.

'HELLO . . . be loud, I am not able to hear you,' Rupali's loud voice echoed in the silent dark corridor.

'*Yahaan signal nahi aata. Us taraf jaaiye,*' (The network is weak here, go to that side.) The peon shouted from behind Rupali, pointing his finger in the opposite direction on the same floor.

Rupali followed the instructions in haste.

But by the time she walked down the dark corridor and arrived on the other side of the building, the call had dropped. So she tried to call back. But then, the very next moment she disconnected the call for there was something that had suddenly caught her attention.

In front of her was a window and there was some movement she could detect inside. As the outside was comparatively darker than the inside, Rupali had a clear view without anyone from inside being able to easily notice her. From a narrow gap in between the panes of the window she saw something that shook her.

She saw the back of a lady, who from her dress, appeared

to be a lady peon from the college. She was standing in front of a man who sat on the edge of a table with his feet comfortably touching the ground. Rupali could barely see him. But what was clearly obvious was that he was running his hands over her back, up inside her blouse. The lady peon's body language showed her reluctance. She was trying to pull herself out of the man's grip. Yet she wasn't shouting, but murmuring. She repeatedly tried to pull the man's hand out of her blouse. But the man persisted, clearly pushing himself against her will. For one moment, when the peon managed to step away, Rupali was able to see the face of the man. It was as if her fears had come true.

Prof. Mahajan stretched his hand to grab the peon's arm.

Rupali was scared. She knew she had no business being there and that this could be dangerous for her. She pulled herself back and tried to breathe. Suddenly, she felt a heaviness, as if a wave of nausea hit her. She began sweating profusely and felt as if she was going to throw up.

Was this really happening or could it be a nightmare?

But the peon's low distressed voice told her it was really happening. She took a moment to digest that a highly respected professor of her college was actually forcing himself on a lady peon. A part of her mind told her to run away and forget what she had seen. But then the thought of the lady peon began to bother her and she stopped. It was certain what was happening behind the closed doors and within the walls of the vacant faculty room wasn't an act of mutual choice. She had witnessed the signs of silent and hesitant protests of the peon. And if she walked away, it would haunt her for the rest of her life.

So she thought to herself for a few moments. She recalled her baba's words, 'Stand for what is right and do not let evil persist.' She knew what she was going to do. And when she had made up her mind, she looked here and there and stepped closer to the window again. She was scared of being caught doing what she was about to do. Yet she was determined.

Right then, her phone rang. It was Tanmay again.

'Shit!' she uttered and immediately disconnected the call, and put her phone on silent mode. She quickly sent an SMS to Tanmay telling him that she would call him back in a while.

Rupali, with all her guts, turned back to look through the window. Prof. Mahajan had by now managed to lay the lady down on the table, her sari riding all the way up to her knees. She was still trying to push him away, but the professor being stronger, did not seem to bother. Rupali could hear her pleading with him to leave her alone. But the professor kept telling her that he would let her go very soon and all she had to do was show her willingness.

Outside the window, Rupali quietly put the cellphone between the windowpane and held it at an angle behind the curtains. She then zoomed in on the scene and began recording. For the next couple of minutes she filmed everything that happened inside the room.

The moment the professor unzipped his pants, Rupali realized that she couldn't be a mute spectator any longer. Besides, she wasn't prepared to handle the anticipated visuals. It was time for some action. She already had enough evidence. Now all she had to do was rescue the peon. She knew she had to be discreet.

So she went to the end of the corridor from where she

had come and started walking back towards the same window. This time she made noise with her feet, loud enough to be heard by the people inside the faculty room. She casually tapped on the door and a few windowpanes and faked talking to someone over the phone. She was loud in her fake conversation as well.

'What, you are outside? I am in the building. Why don't you all come here? It will take you a minute. You guys can do the election campaign planning here! No, no, there is no one here. It's absolutely empty,' she said, walking up and down the corridor, making her words audible to the people inside the room.

'Wait. I will come down. Meet me at the ground floor. Bye,' she said.

When she was done, she quietly walked down and waited for a few minutes on the ground floor. She realized that her trick had worked when, the next moment, she saw the frightened peon walking out of the building in haste.

As the lady peon speedily walked out of the building, she looked here and there, as if hoping that no one had seen her. She was continuously wiping her tears. That's when Rupali realized that she too had started crying. But hers were tears of relief. She wanted to stop that lady. She wanted to speak to her; get to know all that she had gone through. She knew she was making a compromise by being in that room with Prof. Mahajan. She wanted to help her. But perhaps that moment wasn't right. Perhaps, she should give her some time, she thought.

And then, at the next moment, a thought struck her—the professor might also want to leave the building and might see her. In panic, she began to run and ran straight into a firm athletic body and a set of arms that tried to help her steady herself. At a sharp turn at the corner of the college block, she suddenly looked up and her eyes met a set of familiar eyes. He was the same senior who had questioned her about the plant.

'S . . . sorry, I'm sorry,' she blurted out as she came to a dead stop.

He looked up at her and then in every direction across the building, as if trying to figure out why she was running. But he didn't ask her anything. Rupali moved away from him and gave a weak smile underneath her moist eyes. He didn't respond. As she walked away fast, she could feel his stare on her back.

'Who is this guy? Why is he always there whenever anything bad happens to me?' she thought to herself.

Seven

It took Rupali nearly a week to trace that lady peon. She had been looking for her everywhere on the campus since the incident. She wanted to know if she was okay. She wanted to let her know that she was there for her but the lady seemed to have just disappeared. The problem was that without knowing her name or remembering any distinctive features about her, Rupali was having a tough time inquiring about her from the other peons on campus.

One day, she finally found her in the garden area of the campus, where she was busy cleaning. Rupali took a minute to verify if she was the one whom she had seen the other day. There were several other lady peons who wore the same dress but something told her that she was the same woman. When Rupali was somewhat certain, she walked towards her.

'Didi,' she said, addressing her as an elder sister.

In response, she looked up at Rupali questioningly.

Rupali looked at her face and into her eyes. All that she had witnessed a week before flashed through her mind. Swathed behind the poor peon's innocent face, was the pain she had been going through. Rupali was sensitive enough to see that and sympathize with her.

'*Bolo madam ji?*' (Yes, madam?) the peon broke her thought process.

'No need to call me madam. You can call me didi,' Rupali said with a smile.

'*Ji didi,*' the peon acknowledged with a smile. Rupali was happy to see the smile on her face.

'*Kya naam hai aapka?*' (What's your name?) Rupali asked her.

'Ah . . . Raheema,' she replied, wiping the sweat off her forehead.

Rupali, in turn, introduced herself. She then asked her if she ever came to the hostel building. Raheema replied that she seldom visited the hostel block, as her duties were limited to the college block only. But she did ask Rupali the reason for her query.

Not sure about how to initiate the difficult conversation, Rupali lied. She told her that she had been looking for a maid who could do the dusting in her room. It had been more than a month since she had moved into the hostel and now there were spider webs in the corners of the ceiling. She also mentioned about cleaning the cupboard tops and windowpanes and grills. Rupali said that she would like some help with it if possible and the helper would be able to earn something extra at the end of the day.

After knowing the reason, Raheema happily referred her friend to Rupali. She said that one of her friends who worked in the hostel mess also worked for the girls in the hostel after duty hours.

She asked Rupali for her room number so that she could send her friend to her room. Rupali felt a bit disappointed. She needed to talk to this lady and now she wouldn't be able to. So when she was about to pick up her broom from the ground, Rupali held her arm and said, 'No didi, that maid in the hostel doesn't clean well. You come.'

Seeing the way Rupali had held her arm, Raheema felt something different. She wondered if cleaning her room was all that Rupali wanted from her. Yet, listening to Rupali's persistent requests, she agreed to come to her hostel room, but only in the evening, once she had completed her day's work.

Rupali told her that she was absolutely fine with it.

~

'Don't be scared, didi. You can speak freely with me,' Rupali said.

It was evening, and as decided, Raheema was finally in Rupali's room. Saloni had gone off to the basketball court. In her absence, Rupali felt comfortable holding a private conversation with the peon.

Rupali had made Raheema take her chair, while she herself sat on the bed. With her legs crossed and a cushion on her lap, Rupali was continuously persuading the lady to speak up.

'Tell me please, don't be scared,' Rupali insisted one more time.

More than fifteen minutes had passed since Raheema had arrived, but she was not in a position to answer any of Rupali's questions. She looked hesitant and Rupali could understand why. For Raheema, probably one of her worst fears had come true. Her dark secret was no more limited to herself. After all, someone had seen her in a compromising situation with a man, on the very campus where she worked. And that someone was sitting right in front of her and demanding an answer from her.

How does she face this someone? What all did she really see? Was it just as much as she had said—the professor forcing himself upon her? Would this someone ever understand her state of mind now, and more importantly then, when she was being molested? How is she, Raheema, any different from the other women who sell their bodies in return for money, which she had been doing in return for the favour that Mahajan had once done her? Scores of such questions clouded her mind and she didn't have an answer to any of them. Whatever it was, at that moment, she wasn't prepared to hold any conversation with the girl who was privy to her life's closely guarded secret. In her mind, she believed she was the culprit.

Rupali kept on insisting and trying to make her talk. But Raheema was lost in her fearful thoughts. The next time when she heard Rupali's voice and became conscious of where she was, she wondered who all Rupali would have shared this with. For a while, she thought her job in the college had come to an end. The thought of how she would now earn a living and secure a future for her daughter had started bothering her. So she tried to defend her position, even though Rupali hadn't accused her at all.

When she decided to speak up, she only denied all that Rupali had said. She told Rupali that nothing like that had happened and that she might have confused her with some other peon. But her only problem was that her face and body language didn't support her statement. She couldn't look into Rupali's eyes when she spoke. On the contrary, her face had turned red. And she started stammering. At one point, when she could not communicate any further, she wanted to run away. She wanted to run out of that room, that hostel, that very campus. She wished her running away could undo everything.

In a state of panic, she tried to get up from her chair, but Rupali comforted and consoled her. Then, suddenly, she couldn't take it any more and tried to rush out of the room. Rupali jumped out of her bed and held her arms. Raheema's skin felt ice-cold. She was shivering.

Rupali could not think of any other way to stop her, so she hugged her tightly.

'Please let me help you, didi . . .' she pleaded.

Perhaps it was the soothing sound of her voice or the warmth of her body that comforted Raheema. That one moment broke the ice between them. Raheema could not hold back her emotions any longer. She cried her heart out. She gave voice to her emotions when she screamed loudly in Rupali's room. Her unbearable pain gushed out of her eyes. Rupali allowed her to vent her feelings. She continued to hold her body close to her chest and in the tight grip of her arms. She kept rubbing her back gently, allowing her to lighten her heavy heart. For some time, neither of them spoke.

A bit later, Rupali offered Raheema a glass of water. When the two of them sat back again, Rupali was all ears.

'Didi,' she said, clearing her throat. She was finally talking now.

Rupali kept looking at her moist eyes when Raheema started narrating her story.

Raheema was in her late thirties. Yet, for her shapely body and appealing facial features, she made an attractive female in the clan of other lady peons on campus. Rupali had realized this when, earlier in the day, she happened to take a closer look at her. She was a widow and a mother of a fifteen-year-old daughter. She lived in the nearby slums where most of the residents were from her minority community. Years back, she used to work as a domestic help in a few houses, where she would clean utensils and do other household chores. But when, three years back, her husband died of cancer, she had no other option but to look for a better job. On the one hand, she had to run her household and on the other, she had to take care of her daughter's education. Like her, she didn't want her daughter, too, to clean utensils. She had dreamt of a good life for her daughter.

Much before tobacco made Raheema's husband bed-ridden and finally took his life, he used to work as a gardener in the same college. Someone in her community had asked Raheema to see if she could get some work in the college as a replacement for her husband. That's when she had arrived on this campus looking for work.

But getting work, even as a replacement for her husband, wasn't easy. Someone else had filled the vacancy that her husband's absence had created. For days, Raheema moved from one facility office to another, from one security guard to another. At the end of two weeks of useless running and pleading in front of every person, including students, faculty members, the administrative staff and even the security guards, she met Prof. Mahajan.

He had noticed her, probably for the third time, outside the administrative block. Raheema had been standing there for the whole day in anticipation of meeting the facilities manager, who unfortunately, was not even present in his office that day.

Late in the afternoon, Mahajan had stopped by and asked Raheema why she had been standing outside that block for the whole day. She felt obliged that someone of his stature had stopped to listen to her. Raheema told him her story.

Mahajan was a man of great influence. So to get Raheema a peon's job on campus was only the matter of one phone call for him. When Mahajan had told Raheema that she could come to work from the very next day, she could not believe what she had heard. And when it was clear to her, she thanked him scores of times. Back then there were tears of happiness in her eyes.

He was her angel and she would remember him in her prayers—she had said while leaving that day.

Unfortunately, it only took two more weeks for Raheema's angel to transform into a devil. The unexpected had unfolded when Mahajan had specifically asked Raheema to clean his cabin on a holiday, when there was no other faculty member or student in the college block.

Betrayal hurts the most when it comes from the one who you always remembered in your prayers.

It wasn't just Mahajan's hands that clung to her bare waist, but the breaking of her faith in the man whom she treated as her messiah. That night Raheema could not sleep.

In the coming days, Mahajan became bolder. When Raheema stopped at one moment and could not say anything further, Rupali held her hands between her palms.

'Why haven't you reported him to the higher authorities?' she asked her.

In response, Raheema clarified that Mahajan was too big a man for her to take on. He had too much of influence and he was used to getting his way. Nothing was going to happen to him but for sure she would lose her job.

It was extremely distressing for Rupali to know that in order to get a better life for her daughter, Raheema had to sacrifice her life, her modesty.

'But this has to end!' Rupali said firmly.

It was easier said than done. Rupali kept thinking about how she could stop all this and expose the ill deeds of Prof. Mahajan. She was aware that she couldn't live in Rome and fight with the Pope. But then because of the kind of person she was, she couldn't have turned a blind eye to what was happening on campus either. After all, she too had to face Prof. Mahajan. How would she continue to be in his class, in his proximity, when she knew him to be the beast that he was? Moreover, Raheema may not be the only victim, she thought.

She knew that Raheema wouldn't agree to expose Mahajan. She already looked too scared to even take his name in front of her. So how should she go about this, then? All such thoughts occupied her mind when, suddenly, there was a knock on the door.

Raheema immediately got up from her chair. Quickly, she wiped her eyes and tucked a few loose strands of her hair behind her ear. She adjusted her sari and was about to leave when Rupali said, 'Relax! Let me check, you don't worry,' and went ahead to open the door.

It was Saloni, in her sweaty T-shirt and shorts, with a basketball in her hand.

To annoy Rupali, the way she always did, Saloni ran to embrace her roomie.

'Eww! Get off me! You are sweating like a pig!' Rupali shouted while shoving her away.

'*Tabhi to kar rahi hun, meri jaan,*' (That's the reason I am doing this, darling) Saloni chuckled. Then she spotted Raheema and stopped unexpectedly.

She looked at Raheema and then back at Rupali.

'I had called her for some work,' Rupali mentioned even before Saloni had time to ask her.

'All right, didi, you leave now, I will see you tomorrow in college. Keep my mobile number with you. We'll talk later,' Rupali said as she wrote her number on a piece of paper for Raheema.

Saloni watched her go and then jumped at Rupali again. 'You have to listen to what I have to tell you!'

Rupali smiled. Saloni would never let a moment go without bringing some spice into their lives.

Meanwhile, Raheema stepped out of the hostel block. It had gotten dark by then. On a usual day, by this time, she was already home.

All hell broke loose when she arrived at the door of her house. Right in front of her, Mahajan was sitting on a chair and stroking the head of Raheema's daughter, who was busy completing her assignment.

Eight

A week later, the elections were over. The winning party from the previous year had come into power for the second consecutive time. Meanwhile, DU had seen various clashes where the police had to intervene to maintain law and order. On one occasion, it had to take a few students into custody. But that was only for a few hours on the eve of the election as a precautionary measure.

While the elections had gotten over and the peace in the university had been restored, another storm was preparing itself to engulf the college. The signs of it were first felt in Prof. Mahajan's cabin, a day before classes were to resume. That's where the bugle of the battle was blown for the very first time.

'May I come in?' Rupali asked from the entrance of Prof. Mahajan's cabin.

Prof. Mahajan moved his eyes from his laptop to the door and replied, 'I am a bit busy. Come in an hour or so.'

'Sorry sir, but this can't wait,' Rupali responded urgently.

'What's your name, girl?' the professor asked. He certainly didn't like the manner in which Rupali had spoken.

'Rupali Sinha, Sir.'

'Listen, Rupali, I remember you. You had reached out to me for the doubt clarification last week. I was away for a few days. We can discuss that in an hour. Come back later,' he said and raised his hand signalling her to leave.

When Mahajan resumed looking at his laptop, Rupali spoke, 'This is not about my project.'

'Then?' Prof. Mahajan asked in irritation, for Rupali was not allowing him to concentrate on his work.

'Sir, we need to talk,' Rupali said and stepped inside Mahajan's cabin without waiting for his due permission.

Her behaviour annoyed Mahajan. No one had ever dared to speak to him like that. He didn't approve of Rupali's audacity. He shouted, 'How dare you walk into my room without my permission?'

For a second Rupali backed off, but the next minute some inner strength told her to move on. In her mind, Rupali knew what she wanted to do. She had already prepared herself.

She walked towards the professor's desk.

'This is about Raheema. I know what you do to her, Sir,' she said in a calm yet confident voice staring at the teacher's face. Her heart was beating wildly inside her chest.

Prof. Mahajan had heard the name crystal clear without any iota of doubt. His face was something to be looked at. His mouth fell open and in that moment he seemed to be at a loss for words. Being confronted so directly and unexpectedly, Mahajan felt as if he had lost the ground beneath his feet. Clearly, he wasn't prepared for this, not even in his wildest dreams.

All this while, a determined Rupali kept looking straight

into his eyes. She could see the acceptance of wrongdoing in them. Rupali crossed her arms against her chest and waited for Prof. Mahajan to react.

When he got over the surprise, he attempted to ignore the topic. 'Who and what the hell are you talking about? Listen, I am busy. Please come later. Okay?'

In response, Rupali smiled and pointed out, 'Sir, seconds back you were shouting at me. What's made you soft now? Is it the fear that I know what you do to Raheema?'

She hadn't arrived at Mahajan's cabin to leave. She was there to talk. She did not shy away from telling him what she knew. After establishing the facts, she told the professor that they both knew that he was wrong. With a dash of daring she asked him to stop what he had been doing to Raheema, failing which she would have no option but to report the matter to the higher authorities.

'There is no way I will let you exploit poor Raheema any further,' she said firmly, while the professor looked at her, his face red with anger.

Rupali's determination to confront Prof. Mahajan was based on Raheema's agreeing to protest against him. A day before, she had called Rupali's phone and told her that after she had left from Rupali's place that day, she went back home to find the professor there with her daughter. Before she could even think of saying anything, Mahajan had said, 'Your daughter is a good student and willing to learn. While I was waiting for you, I helped her solve a maths problem. If she wants a tutor, I can help her on the weekends. I won't charge a penny to teach her. You can send her to my place.' And he looked back at Raheema, smiling a sleazy smile.

Raheema's blood had boiled seeing Mahajan in her house, running his filthy hand on her daughter's head right in front of her. His lust had now brought him to Raheema's daughter.

'That's it. I can't take it any more! I will do anything to get myself out of this dirty man's clutches.'

Rupali was happy to learn that Raheema had made up her mind to fight. She was equally furious to know the reason for the change in Raheema's stand. Her daughter was the sole reason why she sacrificed her own modesty. As a mother, she would never want her daughter to become her replacement for an animal like Mahajan. And if, God forbid, that happened, then all her sacrifices would be meaningless. She was therefore not left with any other choice.

Prof. Mahajan got up from his chair. He hissed angrily, 'You little upstart! You don't know who I am and what my powers are. Now I will show you what's the result of behaving with your faculty in such a manner. You will have to pay for all these fake allegations you have made against me.'

Rupali stood still and looked at the entrance of the cabin. 'Didi!' she called out.

Raheema appeared at Prof. Mahajan's doorstep. The professor was again shocked to realize that all this while Raheema had been standing outside, listening to what was being talked inside.

'None of my allegations is false. The victim is here. She'll verify my statement,' Rupali said.

'I see . . .' Prof. Mahajan said, looking at both of them. 'So if you bring anyone in my room and convince her to say all that you want her to say, does that prove anything?'

Then he moved towards Raheema and sneered, 'You! Look at you! I helped you get a job here and you are conspiring against me! How dare you!'

'Sir, I want you to say sorry to Raheema and promise us that you will not come in her way ever again,' said Rupali who was now right behind Prof. Mahajan, completely ignoring what he had just said about Raheema.

That further agitated the professor. He turned back and shouted, 'Shut up!'

Pin-drop silence filled the tense space of Mahajan's cabin for a few seconds. Neither of the two ladies spoke.

Raheema was very worried. She wanted all of it to be over soon. She had anticipated that things would unfold like this. But when she was at that very spot, she felt uneasy. Till that day, she had faced Mahajan in a closed chamber, in a privacy that had always made her suffocate. But that day, she was in the open, in the presence of a third person who was willing to fight on her behalf. That day, she raised her voice against the man she had undeniably obeyed for so long. However, that did not take away the latent fear in her heart; the fear of facing Mahajan. And that day, she was not just facing him, but also going against him.

'Who is behind this? Who has sent you two?' Prof. Mahajan turned back and probed, trying to give it a look of conspiracy orchestrated by his political enemies.

Rupali clarified, 'No one is behind us. All we want is that you stop what you have been doing. Else . . .?'

Mahajan cut her short, 'Else! Else what?'

It didn't take Rupali too long to clarify her position. 'Else you will leave us no choice but to report this to the principal and other higher authorities in the university.'

In a state of rage, Prof. Mahajan turned around to stare at Raheema. He was like an injured animal wanting to make his mark. Raheema shrank under his angry gaze. The poor lady didn't have the guts to look at him. She was too scared to even be in that room.

When Mahajan felt that he had overpowered Raheema with his gaze and didn't know what to do next, he turned and walked up to Rupali.

He stood in front of her and looked into her eyes, without saying anything. Rupali matched his stare in response. She saw sheer hatred for her in his eyes. *How could a teacher be so amoral? Weren't they supposed to be even higher than God? Then what made them fall so low?* She thought about what her father had said and that gave her strength, and she stared right back at him with the same hatred he had shown her.

A few seconds passed. But Prof. Mahajan didn't shift his posture and kept staring at Rupali with his furious eyes. His silence was loud.

There were certain moments when Mahajan's proximity and the wrath he showed without uttering anything made Rupali feel uncomfortable. She could hear the raucous breathing of a furious professor who was brashly staring at her. Unable to absorb his anger, Mahajan could have done anything to her. Rupali knew this, but she didn't want to step back either. The heat of that moment was turning Rupali cold. But every time she felt scared, she urged herself to be strong. She kept reminding herself that she shouldn't back off for she was fighting for the right and that it was the professor who should be scared for he was the culprit.

Rupali wanted Prof. Mahajan to speak. She wanted to engage him in a conversation. But with every passing second, Prof. Mahajan was transforming into a beast. His face was turning wild, his eyes red, and his breath louder. It was horrible for Rupali to look at him.

Fearing something unpleasant would happen, Raheema started pleading. But her words failed to register in anyone's mind. At one point, Rupali could feel the sweat on her palms. But she didn't give up. She continued to overcome her fear and managed to hold her eye contact with Prof. Mahajan.

Mahajan began shuffling his gaze between Rupali's eyes. First left, then right, and then left again; in cycles, and then faster cycles. It appeared as if he was going to explode in anger. And then, all of a sudden, the wild dance of his eyes came to rest.

'Else what? Say that again?' he hissed.

Rupali repeated, 'Else, I will have to bring this matter to the principal's notice.'

Mahajan took a moment to digest what he had heard yet again. The next moment he flung his hand in the air. In a split second his palm landed on Rupali's cheek.

The slap resounded in Rupali's eardrums. That was the only thing she could hear in that instant. The impact was so strong that Rupali fell.

Raheema screamed and rushed to help Rupali. When she held Rupali's shoulders, apart from feeling mortified, nothing else registered in her mind. She blamed herself for what had just occurred. In the shock of that moment, she got down on her knees in front of Prof. Mahajan and begged him to pardon her. She cried in front of the professor, pleading that Rupali was just a kid.

Mahajan didn't bother to respond or even look at Raheema. He knew whom he had to break down. He knew who his real enemy was.

When Rupali got back on her feet, she pulled Raheema away from Mahajan, stopping her from pleading in front of him.

She looked back at the professor.

'Go tell the principal now!' Mahajan retorted, picked up his belongings and left.

Nine

'Haven't you understood it yet? The principal won't care enough for it. That dog has slapped you on one cheek, the principal will do so on the other. What will you do then?'

That was Saloni and they were discussing the matter in their room. She was annoyed when she came to know of Rupali's call for action and what had happened in Mahajan's cabin that afternoon. Initially, Rupali had known that Saloni wouldn't understand what she wanted to do, so she didn't want to tell her anything. But she could not lie to her for so long either, especially when Saloni had noticed that one side of her face and her ear were red.

'Are you even listening to what I am saying? You are not going to do anything. Alright?' said Saloni. 'Look at me. You have come here all the way from Patna to study. Don't get into all this. It's not good for you in any way.'

When she didn't hear even a word from her roommate she confronted her. 'Am I making any sense to you?' She raised Rupali's chin and wanted her to respond.

Rupali calmly nodded, only to avoid a debate with her roommate. Saloni too knew that Rupali wasn't buying her argument. She was already extremely disappointed to know what had happened to Rupali. Her roommate's cold reaction to her advice was making her more frustrated.

Saloni's anger was justified. She cared for Rupali and was worried about her; her future; her studies. In her mind, Rupali was the best human she had ever come across and she didn't want to see her ruining her life for someone else. Every time she looked at her red face, in her mind she imagined Prof. Mahajan slapping her best friend. And this was tearing her apart.

A silent Rupali sat on her chair, reflecting upon the course of events in Mahajan's cabin. She was wondering what she was going to do next. One thing was sure in her mind—there was no going back. She was also concerned that Raheema must not retract from her position and must continue to fight this battle that the two of them had begun.

In her anger Saloni walked restlessly in her room. She couldn't contain herself, 'I'm extremely angry with that bastard for having treated you so badly!' she said angrily.

'You hate him because he slapped me. I hate him for what he has been doing to Raheema,' Rupali said calmly, wondering if it made sense to her roommate.

'Raheema! Raheema! Raheema! Why are you so bothered about her?' Saloni shouted in despair.

'Had it been you instead of Raheema, would you have said the same thing?' Rupali countered her friend.

One half of Saloni's mind wanted to respond to that. The other half wanted to understand the gravity of the situation. When she tried to answer that, she realized that she was at a loss for words.

Rupali said again, 'Or had it been my mother in Raheema's place, should I have let the matter be even then?'

'But that's not the case at the moment, right? It isn't your mother. It is the peon whom you hardly knew till a week back,' Saloni argued back but only for the sake of arguing. She knew that she had already lost the argument. She couldn't answer Rupali's previous question.

'Yes, today there is one peon. Tomorrow, there will be two more and they will be asked to compromise or be ready to be thrown out of the system. Do you know the same peon had told me that two years back, there was a student just like us, who had to leave midway because of this monster? No one knows where she went after she left her studies suddenly, or what happened to her. We too are partly responsible for this state of affairs, by not raising our voices against it. If we don't stand up against people like Mahajan, believe me, this one Mahajan will breed more Mahajans. Together, they will increase the number of ill-fated Raheemas in our society. Gradually, people will start accepting the rule of the jungle. If we keep thinking of just ourselves and don't stand up for others, we will always leave the good alone and that's where evil will triumph. Today, Mahajan is doing what he wants because he knows we are alone. But tomorrow, if the entire college is united and shouts outside his cabin, he will be worried and will have to change his ways or better still, leave.'

After a brief pause she added, 'There are moments when we conveniently ignore the logic, just because it works for us. But please understand, Saloni, I cannot do that. I cannot ignore that. That's how I am. What do I do?'

No one could have refuted the honesty with which

Rupali spoke. Saloni didn't know what to say. A few moments of silence were what she needed to understand and digest all that Rupali stood for. There were simply no ifs and buts in the argument. It was the plain naked truth. When you don't fight against evil, you too are to be blamed as much as the evil itself. You have two choices. Accept it, or fight it out.

After listening to Rupali, Saloni's thoughts too began to change. At least Rupali thought so when she did not hear Saloni argue further. She was about to ask Saloni if she had been able to influence her thoughts when Saloni's cellphone interrupted the brief silence.

'Hi baby!' Saloni said but not with her usual level of excitement.

It was Imran on the phone.

'No, I won't be coming today. You guys play,' she said. 'Rupali isn't feeling well, so I am with her. You guys go ahead. I will call you at night. Yeah, bye.'

Rupali looked at Saloni and before she could ask why she wasn't going to play, Saloni came and tightly hugged her roomie. She then kissed her forehead and sat next to her.

'You are so brave!' she said softly but with a lot of pride in her voice for her roommate.

'But not as brave as you to get your boyfriend inside a girls' hostel, that too in broad daylight!' Rupali teased Saloni and smiled to lighten up the mood.

Saloni too tried to smile but the red impression of Mahajan's hand on her friend's face stole her smile.

By morning, Rupali had Saloni's full support. She was convinced that her friend was doing the right thing and therefore she was going to back her in her endeavour. At the same time, Saloni continued to worry about Rupali. She had offered Rupali her father's assistance—he was a renowned advocate in the Delhi High Court. Rupali knew that Saloni was trying to help but she said no to involving him in her fight—at least at that point of time.

However, the more urgent thing to do now was to get dressed quickly.

In the bright morning sun, life was again back to normal in the college block. The classes finally resumed as the elections were over. The hostel mess, where footfall during breakfast had plunged, suddenly witnessed a surge. The demand for paranthas was more than the supply. So a few students simply had the tea and opted to move out and grab a sandwich from the college canteen. The sight of students—in groups and on their own—walking towards the college block in the morning hours, after a break of a few days, appeared delightful. The noisy corridors became a treat to everyone's ears, including those of the faculty. The entire college atmosphere was recharged with energy after the election break. The resumption of classes gave an opportunity to the hostellers and localites to interact, update each other on the news and share a few light moments with each other.

Amid the hustle and bustle in the corridor of their hostel, Rupali and Saloni stepped out of their block to attend the first period, when Raheema bumped into them. Saloni had already seen her once, but by now, she knew of her story as well. Even though she hadn't interacted with Raheema earlier, Saloni felt as if she knew her closely.

Raheema looked as if she had to say something, but

seemed hesitant. Rupali sensed that she was feeling shy in front of Saloni.

'You don't have to worry, didi, she's my best friend. You can speak freely in her presence,' she said, trying to put her at ease.

Raheema gave a weak smile. She didn't look very confident but spoke, 'I want you to meet someone.'

Meet someone? Rupali thought to herself and said, 'Okay, but who is it?' a bit impatiently. She looked at her watch and realized that she was getting late for her class.

'Arjun *bhaiya*,' replied Raheema.

Rupali hadn't heard this name earlier. She wondered who this person was and why Raheema wanted her to meet him. Raheema clarified that Arjun could help the two of them in their battle against Mahajan. But as she was getting late, they decided that they would meet Arjun during the break. They were to meet at Shafi's teashop and not in the college block. She didn't want Mahajan to see her with Rupali.

As soon as their conversation was over, Saloni and Rupali ran towards their college, hoping that they would make it in time for the attendance.

Saloni laughed as they ran.

'What?' Rupali asked.

'Looks like Madam Raheema might be doing a bit of matchmaking here!' she said, naughtily winking at Rupali.

Rupali shook her head. 'You really have a one-track mind!'

Saloni laughed.

Entering their class well in time as the professor was late, Rupali kept thinking about this person Raheema wanted her to meet. 'Well, we shall see who this Robin Hood is!' she thought and started concentrating on the class.

Ten

From the cool darkness of the class, Rupali stepped into the brightness of the corridors and the lawns of the college. She loved the energy of the college and counted her blessings that she was a part of it.

As promised to Raheema, Rupali arrived at Shafi's teashop. Saloni too had wanted to join her and meet the mysterious stranger, but Rupali had said no because if by chance she got late, Saloni could take notes for the both of them.

Outside the college gate, from a distance, she could see Raheema at one of the tables at Shafi's teashop. She was sitting with a guy whose back was towards Rupali. On seeing Rupali, Raheema got up from her seat and waved at her. Rupali smiled and walked towards them.

She arrived at the table and stood behind the guy. She paused for a moment to take off her bag from her shoulder and arrange her dupatta.

Raheema looked at the guy and said, 'Bhaiya, Rupali didi has come.'

The person turned back to look at Rupali.

'Rupali didi, this is Arjun bhaiya.'

Rupali recognized him immediately.

An uncomfortable feeling took over Rupali. She had never thought that the person Raheema wanted her to meet would turn out to be the one whom she had practically hated in her mind. She had no idea how to react to the situation. Since he had been around her the few times she had been in trouble or there had been some problem, she'd started thinking of him as her 'trouble man'!

'Ah . . . hello . . . Sir,' she greeted him shyly. She wished she had inquired more about Arjun from Raheema, before landing up in front of him. Or maybe, at the very least, she should have let Saloni accompany her. How she repented her decision.

Arjun looked at her and smiled as if he had never met her before. 'Please sit,' he said. Rupali took the seat next to Raheema which meant that now she was sitting directly in front of Arjun and looking into his eyes, which made her very uncomfortable.

When Arjun shouted and ordered tea for the ladies, they both refused. Rupali said no a couple of times. But Arjun did not bother to cancel the order. Instead, he asked her if she drank tea. When she nodded, he sat back as if he had proved a point. Shafi added his two bits, 'No one says no to tea when it is ordered by Arjun bhaiya!'

Rupali was very irritated with the statement. But Raheema agreed as a courtesy. Rupali agreed because she was intimidated by his strong personality.

All this while, visions of her initial interactions with Arjun kept flashing in Rupali's mind. She hadn't forgotten the interrogation on her first day on campus by Arjun. To add to it was the mob attack on her music audition day, where she had seen Arjun standing outside the class while his group vandalized the set-up. Now she had a name to associate with that face—Arjun.

It was the first time that she got an opportunity to observe him from across the table they shared. On this day too, Arjun was in front of her in his typical attire—a kurta, a pair of jeans and leather slippers. He had a stubble that suited his face. Arjun was tall and well built. His wheatish skin colour added to his rough and tough looks. His body language was slow and deliberate. His voice commanded attention.

'*Arjun bhaiya Mahajan Sir ko achhey se jaantey hain,*' (Arjun bhaiya knows Mahajan Sir well) Raheema broke into Rupali's silent observation of Arjun. For a second, Rupali felt embarrassed.

'*Didi mein baat karta hun,*' (Didi let me talk) Arjun spoke, cutting off Raheema mid-sentence and took over the conversation with Rupali.

'Hi, I am from second year Arts. I am a localite, meaning I don't live on campus. I am one of the senior members of the political party in opposition in DU,' Arjun introduced himself. 'I have known Raheema didi for more than a year now. I am also aware of the kind of animal Mahajan is. I have a fair idea that he has been creating problems for certain staff members in college. But I am not well versed with the exact matter. What Raheema didi told me last evening is very little for me to understand but I'm wondering why she didn't tell me earlier. Perhaps she was scared of someone. So you give me the details and let's continue to talk in English to save her from embarrassment.'

As he finished, he turned towards Raheema—she was innocently trying to understand their conversation and nodding. He smiled. *'Aapko baad mein batayenge saari baat.'* (We'll tell you everything later.)

She nodded. More strongly this time.

Rupali smiled. That was sweet of Arjun. Then she began to narrate all that had occurred in the past week. At times, she struggled to choose her words. The thought of describing a woman's molestation at the hands of a man to another man, against whom she already had her preconceived notions, bothered her. To add to her difficulty was the presence of Raheema. Just a change of language was not going to make it easier for Rupali. How could she, in her presence, paint Raheema as if she were a toy in Mahajan's hands? How could she tell him that it wasn't a one-off incident, but that Raheema had to fulfil Mahajan's demands whenever he desired? She found it difficult to complete her sentences, appearing at a loss for words. Yet she didn't stop till she finished all she had to say.

Arjun could clearly see her discomfort, but thought it was better not to interrupt.

Poor Raheema, even though she didn't know what exactly they were saying about her, she knew the import of their discussion. She didn't have the courage to look into Arjun's eyes; the same Arjun whom she had called bhaiya all this while. She silently kept sipping the tea that had just been brought.

On the other hand, as the dark secret of what Mahajan used to do to Raheema unfolded, Arjun became restless with anger. Rupali could clearly see Arjun's body language transform. She could see that he had clenched his fists and his eyes had become slits, and he was staring angrily into the distance.

She got scared and stopped.

It took a while for Arjun to notice that Rupali wasn't speaking. When he realized that, instead of looking at Rupali, he turned towards Raheema, who didn't know what to say. In her own eyes, she was the culprit first and then the victim. Somewhere in her conscience she believed this ill fact. The poor lady thought she was equally responsible, as Mahajan, for her fate. She didn't have the guts to face Arjun. She had known Arjun for a long time now. From helping her with money when her daughter had fallen ill, to facilitating her paperwork at the college premises, Arjun, on various occasions has been Raheema's angel. On the other side, there had also been occasions when Arjun had asked Raheema to pray for him, especially during his exams. There had been times when Arjun had visited Raheema's house to break the roza for the day at iftaar. He would eat fruits and puddings that Raheema would specially cook for him.

But while she was wondering about how she would face Arjun now that he knew the truth, Arjun was contemplating the depths to which Mahajan had fallen to molest poor Raheema.

He felt sorry for all that Raheema had gone through and realized that he had really not done anything for her!

'Aap ne mujhe pehle kabhi ye sab kyun nahi bataaya, didi?' (Why didn't you tell me all this before, didi?) he asked softly. He didn't want to scare her away.

Raheema relaxed. Arjun's gesture showed that he cared for her. Suddenly overwhelmed, she could not hold back her tears. In response to Arjun's question, she only joined her hands.

She wanted to say something, but she choked with tears.

Arjun, immediately held her hands and tried to console her. Rupali too got up and reached out to Raheema to help her control her emotions. She rubbed her back and asked her not to cry, and rather face this with strength.

Thankfully, there weren't any other students at Shafi's shop as by then the break was long over. The only people to notice the three of them were Shafi's boys who worked at the teashop.

'*Yeh aap ki galti nahi hai, didi,*' (This is not your fault, didi) Arjun said.

Rupali added to it by reminding her that it was a courageous move on Raheema's part that she had taken a stand to fight against Mahajan. 'I am so proud of you,' she said.

Arjun too agreed. Together they talked about how she probably had had no other choice but to sacrifice her life for the future of her daughter. Instead of letting Raheema feel guilty, the two of them tried to make her feel proud of the sacrifices she had made in her life.

When Raheema continued to sob, Rupali went behind her and took her in her arms.

Raheema looked up at Arjun, who was smiling. Raheema smiled through her tears.

That brought the much-needed closure. Arjun was impressed with Rupali's simplicity and honesty.

Once they were more in control of their emotions they settled down to talk again. Rupali felt that it would be wiser for Arjun and her to talk in Raheema's absence. Arjun agreed. He asked her if they could meet in the evening. Rupali thought for a bit and then agreed.

'Great, so give me your cellphone number?' he asked.

'Uhh . . .' Rupali hesitated. All of a sudden, the idea of sharing her mobile number with someone like Arjun bothered her. Why was he asking her to give him her mobile number? She wondered how to tackle this awkward situation. She hadn't anticipated it. It happened so fast. She wasn't even prepared to react to it. But how would she refuse?

Arjun seemed to have guessed her predicament. 'I am not asking you to share your number. Just take mine, in case you need it before we meet to discuss this,' he said with a smile.

How fast he had read her mind! 'It's not like that,' she said embarrassedly. But Arjun didn't respond. He dictated his number and Rupali saved it.

'Shall we meet by 5.30 in the evening then?' asked Arjun.

'5.30 . . . hmm . . . alright. Shall I come here?' Rupali asked.

'This teashop will be closed in the evening, so we can meet somewhere else. I will see you outside your hostel.'

'Oh! Where exactly outside the hostel?'

'Let's meet at the same place where you had planted that sapling.'

Eleven

'Oh, look at that! Tiny tulsi flowers have blossomed on your plant,' Arjun said while looking at the plant with great amusement. His hands on his waist, he bent down to get a closer look.

Rupali had never imagined such a pleasant reaction from Arjun towards her plant. More than a month and a half earlier, right at the same place, Arjun's face had a different expression when he had first seen Rupali planting that tulsi sapling. She was delighted with this change in his attitude but did not say anything. After all, the disruption he had caused at the music club audition had painted a certain picture of Arjun in her mind. She couldn't have changed it that quickly.

'Yes, it took a while for this to happen,' Rupali nodded. Rupali could have said more.

Perhaps Arjun felt so too. He waited for her to say more. But she didn't. Instead, she continued to look at her plant with great affection.

Arjun suggested, 'Let's sit and talk then.'

'Here on the lawns?' she asked, raising her brows. Her hesitation was clear.

'Too many people in the common room. We don't want anyone to overhear our conversation. Right?' asked Arjun.

With barely any choice left, Rupali had to agree.

'Come on. It's fine,' Arjun insisted.

She felt uncomfortable sitting on the open lawns, in front of her own hostel, where other girls could see her in the company of a guy like Arjun, who was neither from her batch nor from her stream. While it wasn't uncommon for boys and girls to sit on the hostel lawns, it was generally only couples who sat there. Other times, there were mixed groups of girls and boys. In this case, they were neither. *What would they think of her?* 'Will they cook up stories on seeing me with Arjun?' she wondered and her thoughts made her uncomfortable.

'Are you sure Shafi's teashop is shut?' she asked again.

Arjun didn't immediately answer that one. He looked at her face as if deriving some sort of pleasure out of her helplessness.

'You like Shafi's tea that much?' he chuckled.

Rupali first nodded and when she realized he was making fun of her, she shook her head.

That made Arjun laugh. Rupali smiled, embarrassed by her foolishness.

'Yes, it is closed. I checked on my way here. But don't worry, if you are uncomfortable, you can invite your roommate. Raheema didi told me that she is aware of the whole thing. Maybe you will feel more secure if she is around.'

So he knew what she was thinking about! This realization embarrassed Rupali even more. 'Oh no, that's not an issue!' she blurted. But when she sat down, she texted Saloni to come and join her on the lawns.

'You are a brave girl!' Arjun complimented her as they started talking. 'Not many boys would have had the courage to do what you have done, that too against someone like Mahajan.'

'Well, to be honest, I actually fear Mahajan,' she spoke slowly. 'I was scared of stepping inside his cabin and was even more scared when he came and stood by my side, before he . . .' she left that sentence incomplete.

Through Raheema, Arjun already knew that Mahajan had slapped Rupali. He didn't need Rupali to complete her sentence.

'I understand. In fact, that's why I said that you are a brave girl,' Arjun said. Rupali looked at him. 'You see, being brave doesn't mean the lack of fear. It means overcoming your fears. You overcame your fear to challenge someone like Mahajan. More importantly, you did so not for yourself, but for someone else. That is being really strong.'

Rupali felt good. She knew that what she had been doing was right, but no one till then had said the same.

She said, 'There is something else as well that I want to say.'

'Yes?'

Rupali took a deep breath. 'To some extent I'm scared of you, too,' she confessed.

And just after she'd said that, she wondered if it had been the right thing to do. Suddenly, her own words had made her feel uncomfortable again. She felt a strange sense of vulnerability because she was sitting next to the person she was scared of and telling him that she was sacred of him!

'Wha...what? You are scared of me?' Arjun asked, surprised. 'And all because I asked you questions about your plant?'

'Not just that episode, but primarily for what happened on the day of the music club audition.'

'Wait a minute. You were inside the class that evening? Are you a part of the music club?'

'Yes.'

'Oh God!' Arjun exclaimed and looked up at the sky.

None of them realized then how the whole discussion had switched from brainstorming about Raheema's case to discussing personal matters.

'And you believe that . . . Oh God! No . . . No . . . No . . .' Arjun started but then stopped.

Rupali kept looking at him.

'So you are scared of me because you believe I broke and disrupted your set-up?' he repeated.

'I was scared of the whole mob and you were one among them,' Rupali said.

'Okay, I can completely understand how you must have judged me. But the problem is with your interpretation.'

'Why?'

Arjun took a moment and then asked her, 'Did you see me breaking anything or hitting anyone?'

Rupali remembered that she had seen him standing outside the class. She remembered seeing him standing with his arms folded across his chest.

'No.'

'I am glad you said that,' Arjun said. 'Look, I don't know what you will think about me when I tell you this, but hear me out. Yes, those were my party's members. Yes, my party members vandalized the set-up. But that doesn't mean I wanted to do the same. I had protested against any sort of violence. You would have certainly seen me at the venue. But you would not have observed my late arrival. When I heard from one of our volunteers that a few party members had gone to disrupt the audition, I ran to stop them from hitting anyone. But unfortunately, by the time I arrived, it was too late. The damage was done.'

'Really? But I saw you standing outside the room. It appeared to me that all that had happened within the class, had happened under your command!'

'Perhaps then you failed to see the look of helplessness on my face,' Arjun said with a hint of a smile.

'Oh!' Rupali uttered. She realized how the truth could be so different from her own interpretation of it. Arjun appeared honest to her. She believed what she had heard; she didn't want to inquire any further. As she heard Arjun out, her mind was continuously working on building up a new image of Arjun, which if not positive, was definitely neutral and far better than the previous negative one. Her thoughts were broken by the beeping of her cellphone. She picked up the mobile to read an SMS. It was from Saloni.

'In basketball court. Will catch u in n hr darling. Muah :*'

Even though his explanation cleared her perception of Arjun, she was still not completely comfortable with him. She felt it would have been better if Saloni could have joined them. But, at the same time, she was now more in control of the situation.

'So when did you join the club?' Arjun asked.

'Hmm?' Rupali was lost in her thoughts.

'Club. The music club,' he clarified.

'Oh! I joined last month only,' she replied.

'You sing?'

'Yes,' she said. Rupali realized from his tone that he wasn't very happy to know that she was in the music club. 'Why? What happened?' Arjun took a deep breath and was about to say something, when Rupali spoke, 'Your party has some old issue with the club, right?'

'Well, unfortunately that is the case. We have some unsettled business.'

Rupali didn't like what Arjun said. It bothered her. She knew of the 'unsettled business' as Tenzing had already told her about it. So she understood where Arjun was coming from. Even though she wanted to change Arjun's opinion about this matter, she didn't want to get into that discussion at the moment.

'I only hope that you don't settle your unsettled business by hurting them,' she said and then immediately corrected herself, 'I mean us.'

Arjun looked into her eyes, 'Don't worry, we don't hurt people. No one will hurt you.' Then he changed the topic and asked Rupali to brief him about Raheema's case from where they had left off at Shafi's teashop.

Rupali talked about all the things she couldn't have spoken about in Raheema's presence. At times, Arjun asked questions which Rupali answered in detail.

After Rupali had said all that she had to say, she asked him, 'How do we go further from here?'

'Mahajan is a beast. Are you sure you want to do something about it?' he asked bluntly to understand Rupali's commitment.

'Earlier it was about Raheema alone. Now that he has

slapped me, I have one more reason to take this up,' she said with quiet determination. 'However, I want to know why you want to help us on this.'

'I too have more than one reason. I treat Raheema like a sister . . .'

'What if it was someone else in her place, then?'

'I was coming to that. As I said, I have more than one reason. The primary reason is Mahajan.'

She waited for him to explain.

'Mahajan is like a cancer in our college system. A lot of wrong things are flourishing in this university—the back-door admission of a few students, the upsurge in the demand to increase reservation quotas. It is all Mahajan's doing. He has a strong hold on this university and the political backing of the party in power in the campus as well as in the state.'

Unable to connect the dots, Rupali spoke, 'I am not sure if I get it. How does that concern you?'

'I am talking about corruption. Mahajan is corrupt and powerful, now more than ever. Teaching accounts in this college is just a facade. Behind this veil of teaching, he fulfils his personal interests. He makes money by giving admission to those students who are low on merit but belong to highly influential families. He uses the various quotas like OBC and SC/ST to his benefit. From getting fake caste certificates for students, to making them eligible to use the respective quotas, he gets everything done for them.

'Apart from college donations, a separate donation reaches his home for such exclusive work. When you ask why I am concerned, my answer is—I am the victim of this quota system that was illegally used by Mahajan. Two years back, I was the first person on the Commerce admission waitlist. I never made it to my preferred stream but was made to settle for Arts. The reason being, my seat was traded to admit a bureaucrat's son whose Class XII percentage was way lower than mine; all this in the name of bullshit quota!'

'Oh God!' exclaimed Rupali in disbelief. 'But why didn't the higher authorities take some action against him? Are they corrupt too?'

'Not everyone. But some definitely are. But not being corrupt doesn't mean they are against corruption either,' Arjun replied.

'Now what does that mean?'

Arjun explained, 'The real problem is, those who aren't corrupt themselves, don't always fight against corruption. Because they fear that if they raise their voices, they will lose their jobs. Even though such transaction happens under their noses, and they keep their mouths shut. And why would they fight, when they already know the outcome! Corruption didn't take birth in this university. We were introduced to it by the system outside this campus. You see, the college is funded by the government. So if a politician in power wants to have his say and admit a particular student, how would a top college official refuse? And when this wish comes along with cash, why would they? That's where the system gives birth to parasites like Mahajan, who master the art of selling merit for money.'

All this appeared so new to Rupali. She had never imagined that such a sick admission system would prevail within the walls of such a prestigious college. For a moment, she felt disappointed to have become a part of this college.

But Arjun pointed out that the story was the same in many other colleges. He told Rupali that this is what he and his party had been fighting against.

'Two years back, our party had an important agenda of removing the reservation quota. We won the elections based on the issues that we brought to the table. Mahajan's modus operandi was to illegally use the quota system to admit his preferred students. Removing quota would have made it extremely difficult for him to perpetrate his act. Also, back then there was a wave in favour of anti-reservation, supported by those who got admitted through the general category. As per our manifesto, we wanted to eradicate all sorts of OBC and SC/ST quotas. But that's when Mahajan played his game. From creating government pressure to taking the matter to court and getting a stay order, he did almost everything he could.

'Not only this, but he also encouraged various OBCs and SC/ST groups in colleges across this university to fight for their cause. He made himself a messiah of students from backward classes. We continued to fight the battle of abolishing the quota system. But by the time the next elections came, Mahajan had already lured students to his side. He took the backward community students into confidence and asked them to vote for his preferred party. On behalf of that party, he ideated a few populist policies like free Internet in every hostel room and introducing a cheaper student pass for the local metro. Our issue-based manifesto lost to the populist manifesto that Mahajan had smartly carved out for our opponents. Ever since, our opponents are in power and no one has talked about the reservation issue. In fact, as per rumours, Mahajan is working on setting up a domiciliary quota. Most of the influential people in his circle live in Delhi and a domiciliary quota will ease his work manifold.'

Rupali was shocked. She knew there was more to all this but only now did she realize how mistaken she had been to think of lodging an official complaint against Mahajan to the higher authorities of her college. If she did that, she, too, like the others in the past, would be thrown out of the system. But then, what could she do about it?

'So is there no way for us to take this matter forward?' she asked Arjun.

'Not unless we have strong evidence,' he answered.

'The victim herself is the evidence. I have seen Mahajan sexually abuse her. I am the evidence,' Rupali said loudly.

'I understand that, Rupali. But I am wondering how strong our case is with just the two of you on one side against someone like Mahajan. What if Mahajan sues both of you for defaming him? What stops him from saying that the two of you have attempted to malign his image for your personal benefit? What will you do then?'

Rupali argued, 'If he sues me, then I will fight back. What sort of a hidden agenda can be important enough for a woman to put her own self-respect at stake for it?'

'You and I feel that. But in the court of law, feelings do not matter. Facts and the motives do.'

She wanted to counter that one, but with her limited knowledge of the legal system, she didn't have words in her favour. 'But this is not right. You know it. This is not right. It can't keep going on this way. Because, this is not right . . .' she said in sheer frustration.

Arjun wanted to pacify her, but didn't know what to do. He chose to keep silent. Meanwhile, in his mind, he was analysing the strengths and weaknesses of the case at hand and their position to fight it. The thought of reaching out to the vice-chancellor of the university had also crossed his mind. He knew that the vice-chancellor was a lady of values and a person of good heart. He had interacted with her in the past. But he also knew her limited powers on matters such as this, which raised a finger against the powerful nexus in the system. He wasn't sure she was strong enough to break through that. Yet he continued to weigh the odds.

The streetlights in the hostel block and the campus in front were turned on. It had been more than an hour that the two of them had been together. He looked at Rupali and wondered if she was still uncomfortable sitting with him. Probably not—he thought to himself.

Then all of a sudden, something struck Rupali, 'I have evidence!' she smiled.

Arjun was curious. He waited for Rupali to speak.

'I have . . .' Rupali stopped as soon as she began her sentence. She took a second or two to speak again. As she was about to say it, she realized she couldn't look into Arjun's eyes while revealing what she was about to.

'A video of Mahajan sexually abusing Raheema will definitely serve as evidence. Right?'

Twelve

'Shall I?'

There was a disturbing silence inside the tiny cubicle of the Internet cafe.

In the rest of the rows of that overcrowded, noisy and extremely busy Internet cafe, business continued like every day—movies and video games were being played in the private cubicles. The intermittent noises were mostly complaints about the crawling speed of the Internet and dysfunctional keyboards.

Amidst this, there was an odd silence in one of the cubicles.

'Go for it!' Arjun finally spoke.

There was no looking back for Madhab. No second thought in his calm and composed mind. He knew what he was doing. They all knew what he was doing. He clicked the 'Upload' button. The explorer showed a processing sign. They knew it was going to take a lot of time. Madhab had made them aware of the pathetic Internet speed in that cafe. He was well acquainted with this cafe. In fact, he was the one who chose it. As the explorer continued to process Madhab's upload, everyone held their breath in anticipation.

It had been more than a week since Rupali had told Arjun about Mahajan's video that she had shot on her cellphone. After he had seen it Arjun had used his time to brainstorm on how well he could use the video. It was indeed an extremely strong piece of evidence, one that had the capacity to take down Mahajan if used wisely. He was delighted that Rupali had such a strong proof. Time and again he had complimented her for using her mind and being brave enough to capture Mahajan's act on camera.

However, despite such powerful evidence, there were two challenges Arjun could foresee. First, he didn't want to associate Rupali's name with the video. It would be extremely dangerous for her. The video was bound to invite trouble and it wouldn't be wise to reveal any names, not even a proxy.

But then someone would have to bell the cat. Someone would have to own it and claim to have caught Mahajan red-handed. Who should this person be? Arjun wondered.

The second challenge he was worried about was how he could use this clipping to cause maximum damage to Mahajan. Was submitting this video in an official manner to the vice-chancellor the right step? Or was it better not to trust any university authority and straightaway lodge an FIR and then give this proof when needed? But, in both cases, there were high chances that someone in Mahajan's network would alert him much before the truth appeared. Arjun didn't want to give Mahajan time to react.

All his questions found an answer when Arjun got Rupali's consent to involve his close party workers in this matter—the ones he could trust.

Madhab, a diligent volunteer from Arjun's party had an interest in ethical hacking. Had he not been an Arts student in DU, he would have been a network engineer. Prosonjeet, who too was an ardent party member, had been to jail a couple of times during the past election seasons. His experience had got him quite a few connections in the police. Rupali was scared when Arjun first introduced Prosonjeet to her, but had become okay when Arjun had pointed out the reasons for which Prosonjeet had been booked in the past—holding college strikes, organizing mass protests as peaceful as a candlelight march and as loud and vociferous as to disrupt a few political events on campus.

'I have been a political prisoner you see. No extortion or murder so far!' he had said and everyone had laughed.

'Look at his tummy, can you believe this fat ass, a year back, had sat on a hunger strike?' Arjun asked.

Madhab had added, 'And in the evenings he would crave for prawn curry, but settle for cheap fish fry. Drama king!'

Rupali had laughed like crazy while Prosonjeet had made a face. He didn't like it that his good friends were revealing his secrets.

Rupali had asked Saloni to join in. She knew that she would feel more comfortable with her roomie around in the company of the new guys. Saloni too was eager to join them. She wanted to make sure that Arjun did not use her innocent roomie to take revenge on Mahajan.

And that evening, when the five of them had first met each other on the college rooftop, Arjun attempted to establish trust among all of them. He knew how important it was that none of them leaked out any information and each one maintained secrecy. So while explaining the matter to his party workers, who were also his close associates, he hadn't forgotten to include Saloni, giving her the feeling that she too was an important part of the mission. After he had explained the gravity of the situation in great detail and the risks associated with it, he had let the team, including Madhab and Prosonjeet, watch the video.

Unlike Prosonjeet, who had mischievously enjoyed watching Mahajan's aroused expressions, Madhab was disturbed when he saw his cheap animal instincts. 'Disgusting bastard! His wife should see this!' he had said in anguish.

'She will anyhow get to know if we play our cards right,' Arjun had said, after which he talked about the possible challenges. Listening to his concerns, everyone had agreed with him that it would be best not to name anyone as the owner of the video. In order to find a solution, they had first come up with the idea of making a CD and sending it by post to the vice-chancellor's office with a note attached. But there were a few apprehensions. The biggest being—would the VC even act on it?

That's when Prosonjeet had played Sherlock Holmes and suggested what he believed was a brilliant idea. 'Create an anonymous account and post this on the Internet. YouTube, Facebook, Twitter, everywhere! It's that simple! Then we need to make sure a few people from the college watch it, bas! I can bet, it will go viral in no time!'

Everyone was quiet for a while, mulling over the idea. Then Arjun spoke, 'That sounds good! Really good! I think it addresses both the challenges: It promises to keep us anonymous and if we, through an anonymous ID, post this on our college's Facebook group, it will definitely go viral. And something like this going viral on a public domain is bound to create maximum damage! Very clever, Prosonjeet!'

Prosonjeet smiled like he had won a competition. He looked around gloatingly at his friends. Saloni and Rupali too had congratulated Prosonjeet on this master stroke of an idea. But Madhab was still quiet. He had something else on his mind. When Arjun noticed his thoughtfulness he asked him his concerns. Madhab pointed out an important issue in the video. To show them what he was talking about he asked Arjun to replay the video.

Everyone had surrounded the mobile phone, to see what Madhab was going to talk about. Just before the clip was to end, Madhab asked Arjun to pause it. He said, 'See, this is almost a two-minute-long video. Raheema's face isn't visible till this point. But her face is prominent in the last few seconds. If we post this video online she too will get exposed. We can't reveal her identity. This portion will have to be deleted.'

Rupali immediately agreed, 'We can't put Raheema's identity at stake.'

'Don't worry, I will cut it down,' Madhab said. He also explained the precaution that they would need to take before they posted it. 'In case we want to remain anonymous, we would have to make sure that we do not post this from a private device, nor do we use a network that can be tracked. But before that I will ensure that a DVD of this video goes to a local TV channel. We need the publicity but we also need to confuse people about the source of this video as far as possible.' That was an ethical hacker talking. He was well aware of how to play safe with IT networks. He knew how to be cautious and give confusing leads.

By the time they were ready to leave the rooftop, Madhab had planned everything. It was his idea that they would upload the video from an Internet cafe in a remote location in outer Delhi. He had informed the others that it was a busy cafe and in spite of the regulations no one asked for any ID proof and there were no CCTV cameras to track anyone.

Everyone was amazed at how wonderfully Madhab had put it together with such attention to detail.

And here they were, finally looking at the video getting uploaded in this overcrowded dirty cafe where no records of any sort were maintained and they could not be tracked.

The processing bar finally reached the end. Just below it, the message flashed: '100% complete'.

'It's done, guys!' Madhab said. His eyes were still focused on the screen as he refreshed the page to double-check that the video was up for views.

It indeed was.

A chill ran down everyone's spines. With the upload completed, their anxiety had multiplied manifold. They understood the enormity of what they had just done and also of their expectations. They knew the risks associated with it. At best, they had calculated them and reduced them to a large extent. Yet no one could deny that there were always undetected loopholes and unintentional evidence that, if connected, could reveal the truth.

There was silence as they let the moment sink in, followed by a collective sigh.

Sensing everyone's anxious mood Arjun playfully held Madhab by the shoulders and patted him on his back. 'Well done guys! We've done it!'

Madhab turned to look at Arjun. He didn't say anything in response for a moment. Then he grinned naughtily and everyone cheered. They congratulated each other.

Gradually, their fears were replaced by a sense of achievement. Their anxiety gave way to euphoria. All of them felt a sense of companionship.

'Bastard Mahajan will now get it!' Prosonjeet said in excitement. He high-fived with Arjun and then with every one of them in the cubicle.

'True! Now it is only a matter of time,' Saloni said with joy. Everyone agreed.

When the gang arrived back on campus, they hung out for a while before they dispersed. Given the enormity of the moment, Arjun spoke a few words, 'Guys we have done something great today. This was necessary. It is natural to feel a sense of fear, because we have done something secretly and also because we have stood against a powerful devil. But also understand, guys, that we have taken the best approach. We have done enough to mitigate our risks. The best way to put our fears to rest is by thinking that Mahajan wasn't afraid of anyone before doing all the wrongs that he did. So why should we be afraid of doing the right thing?'

Arjun's words not only comforted everyone but also rekindled their determination to fight against Mahajan. Their apprehensions had been taken care of and they were optimistic about the outcome.

Rupali was happy. Even though she hadn't spoken, she appreciated Arjun's leadership skills. She knew that it wasn't the end of her fight for Raheema, but she reckoned that with Arjun's help she had come a long way. Besides, it wasn't only her fight now, she had friends on her side as well.

Soon, the five of them dispersed.

Back in their individual spaces, they waited to see the fruits of the seeds they had sown. The IT geek Madhab was the first to check the progress. As soon as he went online, he realized that Saloni was wrong when she had said that it was only a matter of time before the video would go viral.

It had taken no time at all.

Thirteen

There are fires that spread gradually. Then there are those fires that spread in no time. They offer no time to douse them and burn everything that comes in their way. The fire in DU, with Mahajan, the accounts professor, as its epicentre, was of the second type.

The extent to which things got raked up by the end of the next week was unimaginable, even to the ones who had started it. It was as if the university world had been waiting for the evidence. With anonymous, yet strong facts pointing towards Mahajan, luck seemed to have disowned him completely.

The morning after the video was uploaded on the Internet, Mahajan was the talk of the campus gatherings and discussions. A few tech-savvy youngsters had anticipated that with the number of views of the video over the Internet growing so fast, the sites might verify the content and pull it off. To overcome that, they recorded the video stream on to their devices. That's how it moved from the Internet to cellphones. And then from one cellphone to another.

From the college's Facebook page, the video made its way

to DU's Facebook page. It then landed into alumni networks from where it got pushed into their respective corporate circles. Its final destination was the news channels, where it became 'Breaking News'. It wasn't broadcast, but had become the subject of prime-time debate.

The sky had fallen over Mahajan's head. Below his feet the earth too had moved. It was as if a calamity had engulfed him from all directions and he had nowhere to run. As if with passing time, misfortune was tightening its grip on him and was now preparing to swallow him.

Mahajan was not left with any time to investigate who was behind all this. Though he had a fair hunch that it might have been Rupali who, his followers had told him, had been seen with Raheema and Arjun. But there was no time to investigate that. Additionally, a local TV channel, for the sake of TRPs, claimed it as their own 'sting operation'. Clearly Madhab's idea of making a DVD and shipping it to that local channel had worked towards confusing the media and the public.

The letter that he posted along with the DVD had read:

'This is a genuine recording. If you don't believe it, then wait till tomorrow. It will be all over the Internet. Feel free to claim this recording and then break the story on your news channel. Don't attempt to find out who I am.

A well-wisher of your channel.'

The channel, a sycophant of the party in opposition in the state, knew how to use every opportunity against the party in power. When backed by its promoters, the channel lambasted Mahajan, who was the ruling party's right-hand man in DU, without giving it a second thought.

When one channel broke the story, others too wanted to

play up the hype. Without investigating the source, they simply ran a ticker claiming that 'The channel doesn't vouch for the authenticity of the video', and went ahead with Mahajan's character assassination, debating how the whole education system had become corrupt.

Guided by the national media, there was public pressure not only to sack Mahajan but also to book him and throw him behind bars. In the normal course of the law for the latter to happen, an FIR had to be lodged. But without the victim coming forward, the question was—who would lodge the FIR? The opposition party leaders were willing. Clearly, they were more interested in playing opportunistic politics and weeding out Mahajan from the system. However, everyone believed that if the actual victim didn't turn up and made a statement, it would only become a fragile case against Mahajan. So they appealed time and again for the victim to turn up.

In next three days, seven women turned up. They claimed to be the woman in the video. It turned out that all of them were fake—women bought by opposition party leaders only to start the proceedings. They were soon dismissed when the evidence did not coincide with what was being shown. Some women did not have the same physical appearance as the woman in the video. Some weren't able to prove that they were on DU's payroll. They also could not prove how they landed up inside the DU campus on the given day. The video had a date stamp.

Arjun and Rupali had never thought that what they had done would lead to a controversy of this magnitude. Everything they heard of and got to know came through public sources. No one knew about their hand behind all this. Rupali and her gang seamlessly mixed in the crowd protesting against Mahajan, as if they were just like them—people who first saw the video on the Internet. But the story of fake victims turning up to file the FIR bothered Rupali more than anyone else. Arjun had told her that if this continued, it would dilute such a strong case and only lead Mahajan to prove that all this was a conspiracy against him.

Because of the enormous interest the case had generated, and for the sake of his daughter Saloni, the renowned lawyer of the Delhi High Court, Kailash Chadda, came forward to help them. This happened when Saloni had gone home and told her father the truth. Instead of being angry with his daughter for jumping into this mess, he had supported her. He believed that she had, for the first time, taken a great stand in her life. He didn't want to let her down. He'd therefore called Rupali and her newfound gang to his premises to talk to them. He told them of ways in which they can get away without making the victim file an FIR. There is a provision that any independent citizen of this country can step forward and lodge an FIR, he explained. And with the evidence in the public domain, it's a lot easier to do so, he had said. That's all one needs to kick-start the process. The victim is needed at a later stage when the court case begins.

'But unfortunately the society we live in, unless one has some incentives he or she wouldn't do so,' he added.

But he also promised his daughter that once the FIR is filed, he would make sure that Mahajan is immediately booked and sent behind bars and then he will move court against him.

The very next day, a formal FIR was lodged in the police station of North Campus.

Once strong, the Mighty Mahajan, had now become a rat who didn't dare step out of his house. Bad times are the true test of people who care for you. Sadly for Mahajan, there was no one to back him up. His wife had left him and gone home with the kids. Politically, too, he had been abandoned. Why would anyone want to sail on a sinking ship? For his political masters, instead of facing the issue it was a chance to sacrifice Mahajan and gain brownie points in the name of sympathy for women. And that's what happened.

By the end of a weeklong public protest after the video was first posted, backed by strong media support, the opposition party's demand and finally an FIR, Mahajan was arrested. A warrant had been issued against him in the high court. For that entire week, thankfully for Rupali and Arjun, nothing else happened in the country that took away the limelight from this issue. In various forums, in debates, in the media, the 'University Account Professor's Secret Class' continued to be the topic of much discussion and anger towards the system.

The university, in one of its official statements, had announced the sacking of Mahajan. They were now looking for his replacement. Meanwhile, Mahajan in his misery, got busy moving to and fro between the court and the lock-up.

'But one thing is not clear. Who would have lodged the FIR?' Prosonjeet asked out of sheer curiosity. The newfound gang was celebrating their victory on the college rooftop.

'Yes, even I was wondering the same,' Saloni repeated.

'May be one of the victims of Mahajan's ill acts from the past? Anyway, we will get to know by tomorrow. For what this case has become now, it can't remain a secret. Someone will break the story,' Arjun said.

'I lodged the FIR.'

Those words from Rupali stunned everyone. It took a moment for everyone to absorb this new bit of information.

'What?' Saloni said stepping closer to her roommate. She further held her shoulders.

'Why did you do that?' Arjun asked, his voice full of worry. He was worried about Rupali revealing her identity and taking Mahajan head on in the public sphere.

'Why didn't you ask me first?' Saloni shook her shoulders.

Everyone waited for Rupali to speak up. And so she did.

'I lodged this FIR in the capacity of an independent citizen of this country, just as your father suggested,' she said looking at her roommate. Saloni was about to say something, but Rupali cut her off mid-sentence and continued to say, 'If I would have asked you before doing so, I know you would have tried to stop me.'

The boys continued to listen in a state of surprise, while Rupali continued to clarify the matter.

'In my FIR I haven't claimed that I shot the video. I am not the victim as well. I just lodged an FIR based solely on the evidence in the public domain. No one really knows who actually shot the video and who uploaded the same. Our identities are still hidden. The world continues to believe it was that local TV channel. Many also believe that it's a bunch of mischievous students. After what your father said, I kept thinking the whole night. And then this morning when I knew what I was going to do, I called up my baba. I didn't want to do this without taking him into confidence.

I explained to him all that had happened and my stand on this subject. It was only after about an hour-long discussion that he was convinced that I was right and I should do what I believed in. He said he is with me. I explained to him that I didn't want to see Mahajan playing the victim card and make it seem like a conspiracy against him. I didn't want him to escape. I also clarified that filling an FIR is only a mental block. When the evidence is in the public domain, filling an FIR against the culprit is merely a formality.' She paused for a moment and then finished by saying, 'Besides, I had to settle my equation with Mahajan. He had slapped me in his cabin. He should know that it's my turn to even it.'

'So you slapped him in public!' Prosonjeet clapped appreciating Rupali's guts. It changed everyone's perspective.

The next morning DU acknowledged Rupali as its hero.

Fourteen

That day the first semester exams had got over. While Rupali believed that she had done fairly well in the rest of the subjects, it was statistics that hadn't gone as per her expectations. But that wasn't the reason behind her emotional state of mind that afternoon after writing her final test paper.

Scores of auto-rickshaws had lined up outside the campus and awaited their turn to drive inside the hostel. There was a constant stream of students coming out with their backpacks and rucksacks. Their faces radiated immense happiness. The joy of going back to their homes in the semester break was clearly visible on each and every face. Far away from the world of books and classes, celebrating Christmas and New Year's with the family was on everyone's mind.

The entire university awaits the winter break but no one more than the first year batch.

While they were waiting for their ride, they briefly discussed how the last exam had gone. They also chatted about who was going where, by which train and when they were planning to come back.

Most of them were to travel in groups, while some had

to go alone. As they bid goodbye to each other, the auto-rickshaws drove them out of the hostel.

But unfortunately, unlike others, Rupali was not going back to her home town. The sudden news of a car accident in her extended paternal family had totally changed her vacation plans. The news of her relatives admitted in the ICU at a hospital in Kolkata had made her parents rush immediately to attend to the injured. They boarded the next available train. Tanmay too had left with them. With no immediate family members in Patna, it was meaningless for Rupali to go home. Moreover, with such short notice, there were no seats available in trains from Delhi to Kolkata. Rupali had no choice but to stay back in Delhi.

Seeing off her batchmates and watching them leave the campus one by one, had left her sad. Just like them, she too wanted the joy of going back to her home town and spending the holidays with her family.

She watched Saloni pack her bags too. Her family had planned a two-week holiday in Australia. She was going to join them. For the sake of giving her roomie company for a little more time, she had asked her father to send the driver late in the evening.

They chatted happily about the college and their friends as the two of them stepped out and walked towards the mess. And just like that, Rupali turned around to look at their hostel block. Unlike other evenings, now only a handful of rooms were lit against the dark evening sky. She sighed. She could actually count them on her fingers.

But Saloni tried to sound happy. 'See, you are not alone. You have company!' She said, trying to comfort her friend.

Rupali didn't say anything. She checked if any of the rooms on her floor were lit. There were none.

Inside the mess the scene was similar. There was no one at the dinner table. Rupali picked up a tray and took some dal and a chapatti. Saloni said she wasn't hungry. She said she would take a bite or two from Rupali's plate. She was going home as it is and her family would be waiting to eat dinner with her. They sat at one corner of the table. Even though she had company, Rupali couldn't eat anything. How desolate the noisy mess had turned into! she kept thinking.

Soon another group of girls came into the mess. Saloni identified that two of them were from the third year batch and played basketball with her. She spoke to them and also introduced her roomie. The girls were not going back home and were going to stay back at the hostel for the entire holidays. They said it was fun staying back. They planned to go out for movies and short trips to nearby places.

That was comforting for Rupali. It didn't stop Saloni from asking her senior friends in the basketball team to look after her roommate in her absence. Everyone laughed at that. Rupali felt embarrassed. Saloni laughed too, but said she was serious.

While they were talking, three more girls from the first year entered the mess. They were from the Arts stream. Rupali didn't know their names, but recognized them by face.

She was the first to ask them, 'Not going home?'

'No,' they said as they shook their heads.

Rupali was selfishly happy. She did not want to be by herself.

All of them chatted on as they ate their dinner. Rupali

felt somewhat happier that she wasn't going to be as alone as she'd thought. Later, when Saloni's car arrived, she hugged her and said goodbye. They promised to be in touch.

~

The next morning Rupali got up early. The unusual calmness in her hostel hadn't let her sleep for long. While she brushed her teeth at the washbasin, she heard a few voices. They weren't from her floor but perhaps a level or two above. When Rupali paid attention to them, she realized they were two maids at different floors talking loudly to each other while cleaning the washrooms. She realized that in her abandoned hostel the voices had now begun to echo. The dark galleries and the still walls of her barren corridors reminded her of being all alone on her floor.

So she stepped out of her block and went to the lawn in front of her room. It was still early morning. The chill in the air made her pull her stole tightly around herself. She shivered slightly as she stepped out, but the cold breeze caressing her face felt good! Her cheeks turned red. She breathed deeply. *It wasn't so bad being alone and she was beginning to enjoy the quiet!*

It was all so peaceful. A pair of parrots landed on one end of the lawn. They were perched delicately on the thin branches of the hedge that ran along the periphery of the lawn. Then they began chirping and hopping around. Rupali watched them attentively. It felt nice to see them. Their chirping soothing, like melody to her ears. It was a change from the usual noise in the hostel. New, beautiful sounds replaced the hullabaloo of the hostel.

She felt like taking off her slippers and walking. She removed one first and stepped on the grass. The dew-laden tiny strands of wet grass tickled her sole. She enjoyed that moment. She then took off her other slipper and placed that foot on the grass, too. She smiled when she felt a fresh tickling sensation. She walked around barefoot, happily exploring the pleasant damp earth underneath her feet and appreciating how beautiful that morning actually was. For a while, she forgot that she had not gone back home.

The chirping of the birds caught her attention again. She turned to look at the two of them. She observed how they jumped from one branch to the other. At times they took a short flight to move to the other side of the hedge. And on some instances, they came looking for something to eat on the ground.

Watching them pecking in the grass, Rupali became curious about what they were eating. She walked towards them to observe them from a closer distance.

But unfortunately, the pair sensed a potential threat in Rupali. Even before Rupali could move closer, the pair flew away.

'Oh wait!' Rupali shouted, her arms raised in their direction while her eyes followed them. She was sad to see them fly away. She shouldn't have disturbed them, she thought sadly. She then looked around to see if there were any more birds to give her company.

She found none.

And that's when her tulsi plant caught her eye. She walked towards it to see how much it had grown. She had been so caught up with her exams that she hadn't found any time to take care of it. It was the gardener who had been watering it and maintaining it along with other plants in the lawns.

Rupali bent down and ran her fingers across the little branches. There were now tiny flowers on their tips. The strong fragrance of tulsi filled her nostrils and she inhaled deeply.

'Ah!' she exclaimed. 'Look how big you have grown!' she said and kept caressing the plant as if it were a little puppy. She'd read somewhere that plants too responded to human touch and grew stronger when they were talked to.

She felt like it was only yesterday, that she had planted it. It was only a little sapling back then. Her thoughts went to Arjun. It seemed like yesterday when she'd first met Arjun at this very place for the first time. She wondered how her perception about him had completely changed. From a senior who she thought was a bully, she now felt that he was a caring person. They had seen a lot of each other and so much had happened in the past six months. She thought about Raheema and her life. How that poor lady had undergone such a miserable life for so long. She wondered how many Raheemas would have lived a similar horrible life, scared to speak up and dying a new death every day. Even though it had been a month since Mahajan was in the lock-up, she still found it difficult to accept how the entire episode had unfolded and had such a favourable ending. She thought she had just got lucky that she had the evidence. But then, in her heart, she also knew that luck follows those who seldom include it in their plans.

The sun was finally up in the east. It had already begun to form a patch of warmth in front of her. She sat on the slightly damp grass and stretched both her legs into the sun. She felt nice when the morning rays fell on her wet feet. Minute green, yellow and brown strands of grass along with dirt clung to the base of her feet. They filled in the gaps of her toes and soiled her soles. She sat back and relaxed. Life had been good so far.

Later in the day, after she had her breakfast, Rupali went to visit a nearby Krishna temple. This was the temple she otherwise used to visit every Sunday. But today she'd felt like visiting it again. It was better than sitting idle. She'd asked a couple of friends if they wanted to go, but all had refused. So she'd started on her own. The temple was hardly any distance from the hostel.

As Rupali walked up the steps of the temple, she felt at peace but a little alone. 'I wish I'd not come alone,' she thought. But just as she was about to take off her shoes, something pleasant happened. She saw a familiar face. He'd spotted her before she saw him and had stopped. She smiled.

It was Arjun.

Fifteen

'You haven't gone back?' Arjun asked as soon as he came near her.

Rupali shook her head. 'No,' she said and smiled. Unexpectedly bumping into Arjun had made her feel a bit happy and relieved.

'Why so?' Arjun asked, while offering a share of his prasad to Rupali.

Rupali told him the reason and then took a bit of the prasad because she knew she would get her share when she went in. And then there was a pause in their conversation. There was nothing to talk about.

'You go ahead and offer your prayers. I'll wait here,' he said suddenly.

'Okay,' she nodded and smiled.

'Don't take too long,' he said. This time with a big grin on his face. And there he stood, exactly as she had seen him for the first time, his arms folded across his chest and his head tilted slightly to the right.

Any other time, Rupali would not have wanted anyone to wait for her. But now that Arjun was the only familiar person at a time when every friend had gone on a holiday, she felt warm and happy that he was there for her.

'Yes, not more than five minutes!' Rupali said and almost ran up the steps.

It's not that Arjun and Rupali hadn't been in touch after the Mahajan episode got over. But then the preparation leaves and semester exams had interrupted their casual interactions. To add to the gap was the fact that Arjun was a localite while Rupali stayed in the hostel.

Rupali kept her word and got back on time. Arjun was busy on a phone call. She waited for him to finish and when Arjun noticed her at the entrance gate, he hung up.

'Here. Take this,' she immediately offered her share of the prasad to him. Arjun smiled and took it.

Then Rupali wondered whether they were going to continue talking at the entrance of the temple or would soon go in different directions. And as if Arjun had read her mind, he asked whether she would like to go to a nearby dhaba. 'I haven't had my breakfast and the cook at the dhaba makes really good paranthas.'

Rupali didn't have any plans for the day, so she didn't mind the idea. But she'd already had her breakfast and said so. 'I've had my breakfast,' she said, making a sorry face.

'Then have a cup of tea. This guy makes very good ginger tea, too!' Arjun said immediately.

She looked up to his face and nodded.

'You love tea, don't you?' he asked as they walked towards the dhaba on a street full of pedestrians and hawkers.

'Yes, how did you know?' she asked, surprised. Adding to the chaos around them were the shouts of the roadside vendors who were offering low-cost items at equally low prices and the noisy customers who still wanted more discounts.

'Just like that,' he said with a naughty twinkle in his eyes.

Rupali stood there, surprised. Arjun didn't seem like an ordinary guy. There was something very warm about him, something that made her feel nice.

'Now are you coming or not?' he asked.

She rushed to be by his side and then they walked together.

'So do you visit this temple every day?' she asked.

'Hmm . . . yes, almost,' he said.

In her mind, Rupali conjured up a new image of Arjun, a religious one.

A gush of hot white steam rising up from the hot bed of a big iron tawa welcomed Rupali to the dhaba. Inside were a dozen plastic tables with chairs on each side. There were a lot of people inside and it appeared to Rupali that everyone was having paranthas! The warm air carried an aroma of freshly made paranthas good enough to tickle anyone's appetite.

Even on a mildly cold morning, the warm air felt nice.

Arjun was greeted by someone at the cash counter. He stopped by for a little chat. Rupali realized that he must have been a frequent customer. By the time Arjun got inside, Rupali had already taken a table.

'I have ordered for gobi paranthas. Are you sure you don't want any?' he asked, pushing his chair back to sit.

'Yes,' Rupali said politely. 'I'll have some tea in a while,' she replied.

'Okay, your choice. You are missing something really good!'

'So how much time do you spend praying every time you visit the temple?' she asked, trying to change the topic. She was curious about how religious a man Arjun was.

'I don't pray,' he said.

'What do you mean you don't pray?'

'I visit the temple because I love the prasad,' he laughed.

Rupali looked at his face. He smiled. She blushed. She had been right. He wasn't an ordinary guy, at least not for her.

Then, thankfully, the food arrived—two hot paranthas with a bowl of curd, a thick slice of butter served separately on translucent paper with some Pachranga pickle.

'Hmm . . .' Arjun stared at his awesome-looking mouth-watering plate. He then peeled out the slice of butter from the paper and dropped it right at the centre of one of the two paranthas. He then sprinkled some black pepper on the curd. In no time, the butter melted and two tiny streams of it ran in two opposite directions.

Rupali watched. She was smiling. The flavour-laden vapours were indeed making it all look delicious. She wondered if she should have ordered one too.

'Hmm . . . delicious!' Arjun said with his eyes closed. His complete focus was on relishing the taste as he took his first bite.

Rupali enjoyed watching him.

'You must have this!' Arjun said the next time he looked at Rupali while trying to dip his next bite in the bowl of curd.

'I would have loved to, but I have already had my breakfast. But next time for sure.' Then she asked again, 'So you visit the temple only for its prasad?'

Arjun nodded, unable to open his mouth which was stuffed with a big bite.

Rupali looked amused.

'Do you know where one can find the best prasad in the entire Delhi?'

'I never ranked temples based on how delicious the prasad served there is!' Rupali answered. She wondered what sort of a daily-temple-going man Arjun actually was!

Arjun licked the tips of his greasy buttery fingers.

Rupali stared.

'Desi food! Desi style! Well, I just can't help it. This whole thing is so addictively delicious!' he said.

Rupali laughed. 'Addictive!'

She could clearly see Arjun's madness about paranthas, so the adjective suited him. As a matter of fact, she sort of liked that childlike happiness in Arjun's nature. She tried to relate this to the Arjun who had helped her fight against Mahajan.

'Bangla Sahib gurudwara,' Arjun said abruptly, breaking her thoughts.

'Sorry. What?'

'The place where you get the best prasad in Delhi, Bangla Sahib gurudwara,' he repeated self-absorbedly.

Rupali slapped her forehead. She was amused at how he still hadn't moved on from the topic of prasads. She found it difficult not to smile.

'So you go to all religious places? I mean you believe in all religions?' she asked curiously.

But Arjun had just stuffed yet another bite into his mouth. Bite by bite both the paranthas had vanished from Arjun's plate. What was left on his butter-coated plate were bits of cauliflower, onions and coriander. They were next on his radar. He stuck his finger on them and licked them off too.

Rupali made a face.

'We shouldn't waste food!' he said mischievously, looking completely satisfied and slumping back in his chair. 'Shall I order tea for you now?' he asked.

'Yes!'

'Great!' Arjun said shouted, *'Bhaiya do chai chahiye aur saath mein ek aur parantha.'* (Two teas and one parantha, please.)

'One more? You are still hungry?' This time Rupali was not so surprised. By now she had a fair idea of what a foodie Arjun was. A man who ranks temples as per the taste of their prasads!

'See, unlike a potato or, for that matter, cheese, cauliflower is a seasonal vegetable. In the winter cauliflower tastes the best. So, since winters will only last for two or three months, it makes sense to eat as many as possible during this time,' Arjun rationalized with his own crazy logic.

Even though she did not buy it, Rupali enjoyed what he was saying. Arjun continued and mentioned mooli and methi paranthas, which too were seasonal. Rupali was quite enlightened with Arjun's expertise on the subject matter that went as deep as mentioning the niche ingredients that one could include in the mixture of various paranthas. Dry pomegranate seeds in aloo paranthas and the slight inclusion of freshly grated ginger in gobi paranthas could take the taste to a different level.

She was impressed. The breakfast back at her place in Bihar was never so rich and calorie-loaded. Not only had she enjoyed watching a man's 'addiction' to paranthas, she had also found out that he had a fine knowledge of the recipes too!

A boy arrived with two glasses of steaming tea and another plate of food with some more butter, curd and pickle. Arjun carefully tore it into two halves to let the steam out.

'Wow! This tea is actually nice,' Rupali said at the first sip of her tea.

'See, I told you, this dhaba is really good. You must try eating this as well,' he said happily and shouted to repeat his order for tea, even before Rupali could say no.

Someone at the counter further shouted out to someone else to fulfil the order. It looked as if it was meant for a barely visible man hidden behind the steam in the makeshift kitchen. Immediately, Rupali stood up, looked at the counter and said embarrassedly, *'Nahi bhaiya, nahi chahiye!'* (No, I don't need any more!)

The counter guy again shouted at some barely visible man, this time to cancel the order.

Arjun laughed.

Rupali sat down and looked at Arjun. 'I can't eat one whole parantha, but can I take a bite from yours?'

Arjun looked at his messed-up plate with patches of curd here and there, and then at his butter-soaked fingers. He thought if he could have eaten like a gentleman instead of demonstrating and justifying his desi style to eat the desi food, he wouldn't have been embarrassed. Now it was too late.

Rupali carefully broke a bite from the parantha where there was less butter and dipped it into the curd in which Arjun had dipped his fingers so many times.

And even though Arjun was embarrassed to let Rupali eat

from his cluttered plate, he loved watching her eat like a lady. He was suddenly very conscious of her presence. Her face was glowing even in the semi-darkness of the room. Her features were delicate—neither too sharp nor too soft—gentle and light. As she ate, a strand of hair fell on her face. She quickly tucked it behind her ear, but now it was shining with oiliness. Arjun kept staring at her. He could feel himself getting attracted to her. She wasn't like any other girl he had known.

Rupali nodded looking at Arjun, appreciating the taste, 'This is good!'

'*Haina*, amazing!' Arjun said, coming out of his thoughts.

Rupali took another sip of tea from her glass and stared at the leftover parantha on Arjun's plate. 'Half–half?' she asked in a delighted voice.

'Just because it's you!' Arjun said, naughtily winking at her and happily sharing whatever was left on the plate.

After what appeared like an hour or so, the two of them finally came out of that place. While washing her hands outside with a jug of water, Rupali suddenly recalled something and shouted at Arjun who was paying at the counter.

'Hey, you haven't yet answered my religion waala question!'

When both of them were back on the street again, Arjun asked, 'You wanted to know if I believe in all religions?'

Rupali nodded.

'Actually, I don't believe in God. I am an atheist,' he clarified.

Rupali was shocked. 'What? So you only go to temples and gurudwaras for free *ka* prasad?' she probed.

The two of them continued to walk leisurely. They hadn't planned where they were going next, so they unmindfully took the way back from where they had come—the temple.

'Firstly, I don't consider it free. Every time I go, I drop some money in the donation box. Even though I don't believe in God, I cannot deny that I feel at peace whenever I come to such places. I have been to churches and mosques as well. Now there one doesn't get to eat prasad. There is a different sort of peace I find at these places. Some sort of a calming effect, that I like experiencing. You see, I don't believe in God, but I like these places.' Arjun tried to explain and was sure that Rupali wouldn't have got exactly what he wanted to say.

Rupali thought it was an interesting argument. Here was a man in front of her, who said he was an atheist, but loved frequenting every religious place. Deciding to carry forward that discussion and wanting to know more about Arjun's thoughts—especially why he was an atheist—she asked him where the two of them were heading.

'No idea, what about you?' he asked and smiled. In his heart, he wanted her to say she wanted to be with him. And even though he had some plans for the day, he didn't mind cancelling them for Rupali. He wanted to know her better.

'No idea . . .' she shook her head cutely.

'Then let's go and taste the best prasad! It will be fun. Have you visited Bangla Sahib gurudwara yet?'

Sixteen

'So tell me, why don't you believe in God?'

They were on board a metro heading towards central Delhi. Unable to find seats, the two of them stood next to each other on the crowded train. While Rupali had rested her back against a vertical bar, Arjun held on to the support hanging above him from the roof of the train.

'In fact, to answer that question, let me first ask you. Why do you believe in God?'

Rupali couldn't give an answer to the question. She had never felt the need to think about a reason to believe in God. It was strange and she only ended up saying, 'Come on! So many people believe in God! If he was not there, why would so many people believe in him?'

'Is that your answer? Because so many people believe in him, therefore you do too?'

Rupali hesitated. 'Yes, that's my reason, because ever since I was a kid, I have been told that there is a God. That's who we pray to at home, and in the temples. Our history establishes this fact. Those ancient holy books in various religions state that there is a God,' she said.

Arjun sighed and shook his head.

Rupali spoke again, 'Okay! Can you dismiss the epics Ramayana and Mahabharata and also deny the presence of Gods in them who killed Kansa and Ravana?'

'Well, a correction, Ms Rupali Sinha,' Arjun said. 'In my understanding, Ram and Krishna were avatars of God and not God themselves. Mohammed was a prophet. Guru Nanak was a guru. They all were messengers of one supreme God.'

'So at least you agree that there exists one supreme God!' Rupali felt she had won the argument. There was a smile on her face.

'Well, I don't deny that.'

'Yes, so when you say you don't deny, it means that you agree. Right?' In her excitement she raised a finger at Arjun. She wanted to nail him down.

'Not denying something doesn't mean agreeing with that thing. It simply means not denying it,' argued Arjun.

'Now you are playing with words,' she pouted sadly.

Sensing that she had suddenly lost her enthusiasm, Arjun changed the discussion. 'Okay, listen. Here are my thoughts. If you would have listened to me carefully, you would remember that I never said that God doesn't exist. I only said that I don't believe in him, which means even if he exists, I do not believe in him. See, I agree that there is something out there, some supreme power that is behind the creation of this universe. While some may call it God, to me it is a black box. I am not sure who or what exactly it is.'

Arjun's point rekindled the interest in Rupali who now happily continued the discussion. Rupali appreciated the fact that Arjun's disbelief in God was not baseless. Irrespective of whether or not he was right, he had a rationale to it. Two people could be equally good even when they may have completely opposite thought processes. Rupali now looked at Arjun with a lot of respect and she couldn't deny she was enjoying his company.

After halting at one of the stations, the metro abruptly started with a massive jerk. Along with the others, Rupali too was thrown off and since she had only rested her back on the vertical bar and wasn't holding on to a support, she was about to fall. To save herself, she reflexively held on to Arjun's kurta.

Rupali, whose first thought after recovering was how to deal with the awkwardness of coming so close to Arjun, tried to move away without looking into his eyes. Suddenly, the trained jerked to a halt again. But she hadn't seen that coming. She was still holding on to Arjun's kurta. Arjun tried to save her this time and, suddenly, the two of them heard a sound of something tearing. It was the chest pocket of Arjun's kurta.

'Oh no! I'm so sorry!' she cried. But she was more embarrassed than sorry. All she wanted to do in that moment was hide her face and never see Arjun till the college opened again!

Arjun looked at his half-torn pocket. He looked at Rupali, whose hand was on her mouth.

'Stop doing that and at least hold on to a support now!' he said laughing.

She looked even more embarrassed.

'Relax! It's okay. You didn't do that on purpose. See, it now complements my ripped jeans!' He chuckled, showing her the patches and threads dangling from his designer jeans.

'No, it's not okay. It looks funny and this is entirely my mistake. And it's bothering me a lot,' she whined.

'If it's bothering you, don't look at it.'

'How do I not look at it? It is right on your chest. Every time I look at you, I look at what I have done,' she answered.

'Then don't look at me.'

'How do I not . . .' and she stopped short of completing it.

Arjun looked at her and then walked away from her. She watched him interact with a few people who sat with their bulky office bags on their laps. She could make out that Arjun was asking them for something. One of them nodded and handed over something from his bag.

It was a stapler.

Arjun stapled his torn pocket. *'Jugaad,'* he said with a smile. 'Does it bother you now, madam?'

'No,' Rupali responded shyly. This caring gesture from Arjun touched her heart, yet again.

Later in the afternoon, the two of them sat in one corner of the sanctorum surrounding the *sarovar* (the holy pool) in the gurudwara. Before arriving there, both had performed *seva* (free services) in the *langar* (free community kitchen) hall. It was Rupali's first time in a gurudwara. Arjun had shown her how in a gurudwara anyone could participate in offering services like storing and polishing the shoes of the visitors, or serving food in the langar or cleaning utensils or the gurudwara complex.

Rupali had joined Arjun in serving the langar and quite enjoyed it. Starting from letting her know that she should keep her head covered to showing her how to serve the chapattis, Arjun had quickly taught her everything. After a few rounds of serving, they ate together. All along, Arjun kept telling Rupali about all that he knew about Sikhism.

Finally, sitting at the edge of the sarovar, Rupali was teasing Arjun on how shamelessly he had taken the prasad for the third time. Arjun kept grinning as he ate the final serving of it with great pleasure.

They sat quietly and enjoyed the calmness of that place. For a while no one spoke anything.

'For all that you do, you are so near to God and still you don't believe in him,' Rupali spoke.

Arjun didn't feel the need to respond. He didn't.

'You do so much here that a God-fearing person like me wouldn't have thought of doing till now.'

'God-fearing?' Arjun asked. 'I thought you believed in him rather than fearing him.'

Rupali was quiet.

Without expecting her to react he said, 'I don't come here to connect with God. I come here because I feel at peace in this divine atmosphere. I like listening to an *azaan* in a mosque, inhaling the smell of incense in a temple, lighting a candle in a church, sitting by the side of a sarovar in a gurudwara. I feel good experiencing all this. That's my only takeaway.'

As they talked, the two of them didn't look at each other. Their eyes stared at the silent waters. It appeared as if they were not talking to each other but to the water in front of them, turn by turn.

'I have never met an interesting person like you, who has crossed the man-made boundaries of religion and still rejects the idea of God,' Rupali said softly without expecting any further arguments from Arjun.

But he responded, 'What's the point of believing in him if he is not there when you need him the most?'

Rupali turned her head towards Arjun and asked, 'What do you mean by that?'

It took Arjun a few moments of silence and Rupali a few moments of anticipation before he spoke again.

'Heard of the Benares bomb blasts in the year 2006?'

'Yes.'

'I lost my elder sister in it.'

'Oh! I am so sorry to hear that!' Rupali could almost understand why Arjun had lost the faith in God.

'She was such a nice human being. She used to help everyone in need and didn't mind sacrificing her time, energy and money for others. Just like you. A lot more religious than me. Yes, back then, I had faith in God—something that I lost after she died in that temple and her dear God, to whom she prayed for ages, couldn't do anything.'

'I can see that you have been holding on to this grudge against God for not saving your sister. But eventually, we will all die one day. Everyone who takes birth has to die. Should one stop believing in God then?'

'Yes, everyone has to die one day. But no one deserves to die that way—in a bomb blast,' Arjun said, looking at her with some rage.

'But it was an act of terrorists. Why are you holding God responsible for it?'

'Because if the world believes that God is that supreme power without whose permission nothing happens, then I have all the right to believe that that very God killed my sister. Yes, that's what I believe.' Arjun sounded rebellious. He pulled his eyes away from Rupali, back to the water.

'Don't say that, Arjun . . .' Rupali softly urged.

'Why not? Wasn't it God's wish? My sister had dreams. She wanted to do a lot of things. She didn't deserve this. What was her fault . . .'

Then he felt Rupali's hand over his right shoulder. Arjun calmed down. 'I am . . . I am sorry.'

Rupali noticed his moist eyes. She gently rubbed his shoulder. 'I don't know if this is true, but our religion says that our destinies are defined by our karma.'

'Yes, it says so. And everyone who knows my sister would vouch for her good karma,' Arjun responded. 'And my lack of faith in God is not just limited to what happened with my sister. Read the newspapers. Little kids who haven't even gained consciousness die cruel deaths. What about their karma? Had they even turned old enough to perform their karma? And if not, then based on which karma did God write their destiny?' he asked.

'We carry forward our karma from our previous lives . . .'

'But isn't this bizarre? How would I know what I have done in my past life? Shouldn't this balance sheet of karma and destiny be settled in one life rather than be carried forward from one to the next? Why reward me or penalize me for what I have done in my past life, which I have absolutely no idea about? Why not do it in this life?'

Rupali looked at Arjun. She wanted to change Arjun's notions on the subject of God, but Arjun ended up challenging her understanding. Her idea was not to win the debate, but to try her bit to make Arjun regain his lost faith.

She looked so miserable that Arjun felt she was going to cry. So he changed the topic.

'And what karma did I do that a girl from DU ended up tearing the pocket of my kurta in a crowded metro?'

Rupali smiled suddenly. 'Don't worry, I will stitch the pocket back,' she said, grinning naughtily.

'Really? I wouldn't mind availing that offer!' he said, laughing.

Rupali nodded confidently. They had a few light moments after that. And after their heavy discussion, these moments by the side of the sarovar appeared like real bliss.

When evening fell they left for the campus. At the gate of the girls' hostel, Arjun bid her goodbye, but not before the two of them had decided when and where they were going to meet the next day.

Seventeen

The holidays were passing by rather quickly for some reason. There was always something new to do. Rupali was enjoying being a tourist in Delhi. One more thing made her very happy—to pick up a topic and discuss and debate it with Arjun. From religions to reservations, from global warming to local mindsets, their agenda had extremely diverse items. Often they would come up with probable solutions to the existing challenges. And the whole exercise of brainstorming became very interesting. At times they were not in agreement and had contradictory views over a subject matter. But interestingly, they never fought to prove I-am-right-and-you-are-wrong. They respected each other's opinions and politely disagreed. It had become a habit for Rupali to jot down the interesting things she learnt from Arjun.

Little did the two realize how the passing days had brought them emotionally close to each other. They would go to places like India Gate and Akshardham and, at times, roam in the markets of Janpath and Sarojini Nagar, randomly buying something for themselves. They would spend an entire day in each other's company. Once out of her hostel in the morning,

Rupali would only come back late in the evening. If there was still some time left for her hostel gates to be locked, the two of them would chit-chat for a few moments next to the lawns; else Arjun would drop her on his bike. Every passing day made them depend on each other's company, so much so, that if they did not see each other for one day they missed each other terribly. They didn't realize this until it happened one day.

Arjun had to go to Karnal to attend a relative's wedding. In his absence, Rupali accepted the invitation to join a few girls from the hostel on their shopping spree, one that she had otherwise said no to. But that didn't comfort her at all! She was used to seeing him every day. All of a sudden, his absence after so many days had left a void that she found difficult to fill.

Miles apart from her in a distant city amid the bustling gathering of a wedding celebration, Arjun, too, felt as if something was incomplete. It appeared unusual to him to not listen to her lively chatter, her lovely innocent voice. With happy faces surrounding him, he wondered what was missing. Why wasn't he happy? Why was he so troubled that he hadn't seen Rupali?

Marriages, music, celebrations, meeting relatives, all these would excite him earlier. He always waited for such events to happen and would get completely involved in the spirit of it. Then why was it that he did not feel like meeting anyone now? Why was it that he was waiting for the ceremonies to get over so he could go back to the same routine with Rupali?

Something had changed for the both of them.

And the only way to tide over this loneliness was to text

each other. So they ended up sending SMSes to each other. To save herself from unwanted attention Rupali had put her mobile phone on the vibration mode. She knew some of the girls she was hanging out with were big-time gossipers.

In the afternoon when Rupali was having a quick meal with her friends in the food court of a mall, Arjun sent a few messages. She thought she would respond after finishing her meal. She also wanted to avoid texting too frequently in front of the other girls.

All this while, however, Arjun kept checking his cellphone in anticipation. He wondered why all of a sudden he had stopped getting responses. It bothered him. He felt he could not concentrate on anything else till Rupali wrote back. It was a strange feeling that was making him impatient.

When he could not wait any longer, he dialled her number.

When Rupali saw his call, she was overjoyed. Her eyes lit up even though she tried to keep her feelings from showing. The other girls noticed and smiled knowingly at each other. Rupali avoided their eyes, excused herself and walked away from them for a bit. Now that was a mistake which confirmed the suspicion of the other girls.

'Hi!' she said nervously.

'Hi!' the voice at the other end responded.

Then there was silence at both ends. A beautiful silence that was pleasant to the ears and that no one wanted to fill. The silence that spoke far beyond just wishes. The silence that gave them butterflies in their stomach.

Arjun, when confronted with this silence, suddenly forgot what he had to say. 'How . . . how are you?' he asked, stuttering, and then bit his tongue. Hadn't he been texting her since he'd left and exchanged at least a hundred messages with her! How beautifully he had put his foot in his mouth with that question!

Rupali secretly laughed at that. She had sensed his discomfort but didn't add to his embarrassment. 'I'm fine. How are things there?' she asked, wanting to know about the wedding celebrations.

'It's all nice, but for some reason I am feeling bored.'

'Bored? But why?'

But Arjun didn't have anything concrete to answer. Rupali too accepted that it wasn't exciting for her to come out shopping with the other girls. She too got bored.

'But why?' this time Arjun asked her.

Rupali had a concrete answer. 'Because they either gossip all the time or only talk about what's in and what's out of fashion,' she said.

Arjun laughed and when he started to say something, Rupali cut him short and said softly, 'I am missing the kind of conversations we have every day . . .'

There was that silence between them again.

Arjun admired her for being upfront and telling him. He wondered if he could have said that to her with such ease. He thought for a moment and then asked, 'So tell me this, had I been there in Delhi, where would we have gone today and what would have been the topic of our discussion?'

'Hmm! Good question. Let me think . . .' she said and then thought for a few seconds before she spoke again. 'I would have liked to go someplace near the airport. I would have loved to see the planes landing and taking off from the airstrip.'

'Interesting! And what would we have been discussing?'

'Hmm…Dreams! Our dreams! Flying high in the limitless sky which is considered as limitless as our thoughts.'

'Looks like we missed what would have been an exciting day!' Arjun chuckled.

'Will you take me there when you are back?' she asked quickly.

The innocence with which Rupali asked that question, touched Arjun's heart. Those soft words 'will you take me', drenched in hope, kept ringing in his ears for a few seconds as he replied, 'I would love to do that!'

A little later, after they hung up, they were again back to the business of exchanging messages over their phones. Rupali was the first one to do so when she wrote: 'It's nice 2 listen 2 ur voice.' When she realized that she had forgotten to add a smiley in the end, she sent a second message, which was just a smiley.

For the rest of the day, they continued to be in touch with each other. They were not sitting idle and were engaged in the company of their friends and family, yet they picked up every possible opportunity to connect with each other. The joyful wait anticipating the arrival of the next message on their phones and the sparkling feeling of writing the next message to be sent, kept them busy the whole day.

By the time night fell and Rupali was about to sleep, Arjun was in a reception. She had bid him goodnight. But sleep was miles away from her. Somewhere, something had changed deep inside her. It was an unusual feeling; she had never felt this way. She had never missed someone like this, not even her family when she had boarded the train in Patna to come to Delhi. Over the past few days, had she developed feelings for Arjun? she thought to herself. Shying away from accepting it she started looking for facts to deny it.

She found none.

She recalled how, earlier in the day, a friend of hers had caught her blushing and smiling to herself when she had come out of the trial room to show her the outfit. Rupali had been lost in her thoughts. For a moment she hadn't even realized that her friend had been asking for her advice on the dress. How embarrassed she had been to know that she had been caught lost in someone's thoughts!

Her interactions with Arjun had been limited to candidly sharing the thoughts in her mind, based on rationale. Since when had this become a matter of the heart? She wondered and immediately rejected her own point. Then why, for the entire day, had she behaved as if she had been addicted to Arjun? When he wasn't there near her, why had she tried to fill in that void by exchanging uncountable SMSes? Her mind and her heart were in conflict, she thought. But the truth was different. They were not. They were in agreement. Both pointing to the same thing, though in a different way. She might not believe it. But that didn't change the truth. And perhaps, for the first time, Rupali had become irrational.

You may fool others, but it is difficult to fool yourself. When Rupali turned on her bed and closed her eyes, rejecting all the hypotheses of there being anything between Arjun and her, she could not control her subconscious mind. It was again thinking about Arjun. It felt nice to think about him, to imagine him in his kurta and a pair of jeans. There was a tickling sensation, a secret joy, of imagining herself with Arjun that led to a smile on her face.

The moment her conscious mind learnt about the thoughts of her subconscious mind, she got up in her bed and, in playful anger, she punched her cushion several times. She sat cross-legged and held her hands over her forehead.

'Why? Why am I not able to think about something else? Why am I not able to sleep?' she talked to herself. Her problem was not that she didn't know the answer. Her problem was that she was not ready to accept it.

When the night would end and the sun would rise again, she was still not going to meet Arjun. He was going to be in Karnal for one more day. Rupali realized with mixed emotions that she was only at the halfway mark and that she would have to wait for another full day before she could see him again. 'After a whole day! Just like that day! Suddenly how difficult it has become to pass thirty-odd hours without him,' she thought. The sadness of waiting for yet another day overshadowed the happiness of having already passed an entire day.

Far away from Rupali, Arjun was still at the reception. His entire day had been full of unplanned, impromptu, last-minute chores and he had intermittently bumped into distant relatives. He danced when he was forced to dance. He drove when he was asked to drive his cousins to the beauty parlour. From monitoring the catering guys to helping the flower man instal the entrance gate, he had done a hell of a lot of work. But all this while he had been constantly in touch with Rupali. The cheerful smile that he had been carrying the whole day was not due to the spirit of the wedding. It was due to him being in constant touch with Rupali. Her frequent messages kept him moving and helped him accomplish things one by one at the wedding.

Late in the night, when his cousins and their friends had forced him to drink a few pegs, for the first time Arjun seriously figured out what his heart wanted. He didn't announce it to his relatives and distant friends. But alcohol had made it evident on his face. They had all seen him continuously texting someone the entire day. In an atmosphere suffused with music, dance and alcohol, the joy of the heart often comes out in the open. But for Arjun, more than anything, that was the moment of self-discovery. With his mind still under the influence of alcohol, it was his heart alone that was talking to him. And he understood what it wanted.

Later that night, about hundred kilometres away from Rupali, a drunk Arjun made up his mind to tell her what he had been feeling about her since morning and, more so, in the past few hours. He didn't intend to propose to her, but just wanted to let her know. He didn't want anything in return but just wanted to be honest. He typed and deleted the text message a few times and then finally stuck to what he had typed at the very first go.

Then, a second before he could send his SMS, his phone battery died.

It is the dawn of December. The darkness at this time of the day is quite pleasant. Rupali is standing at the entrance of the rooftop of her hostel block, where the cemented five-storey-high staircase finally ends. It's cold there. She is continuously rubbing her palms and occasionally blowing on her fingers to keep them warm. She is shivering. She is trying to keep herself warm in the shawl that she has wrapped around herself. Her hands are numb and her teeth are chattering. It's not only the dip in the temperature that is making her tremble like this. It has to do with the reason she is here.

At the entrance, she looks here and there. Far away from her, in every direction, she sees glowing streetlights. It's peaceful everywhere. A few commercial establishments have left their billboard lights turned on. At times Rupali can see a few moving lights—the taxis and lorries moving on the roads of Delhi. But she can't hear the noise of the traffic. They are far away from her. The only sound that persists is the sound of the night.

Up above her, the dark sky looks beautiful. The moon continues to glow, just like it did the night before; but its position in the sky has changed by now. Similar is the case with the constellation of the seven stars. All of a sudden, a bat swings over her head. She pulls herself back reflexively. The next moment, when she recovers her position, she isn't able to trace the bat. It's gone.

She is scared to be here in this isolated place. But she is overcoming her fears and going ahead. She is looking here and there in search of something; or rather someone. The badly illuminated rooftop is making it difficult for her. Some seconds pass. She still hasn't found the one she has been looking for. She is getting impatient. She wants to shout out the name, but fears that someone else will hear her; besides, she doubts if in her terrible condition she would be able to shout. Her teeth continue to chatter.

She knows what exactly is happening to her. It is some sort of anxiety attack; an intense one. Her heart is pounding fast. She needs to calm down but in this moment, she is losing her control over her body. Her body is experiencing goosebumps; one after another in tandem. In tandem they lead to a tickling sensation.

Unable to wait any more, she slides her hand into the pocket of the pyjamas she is wearing. She takes out her mobile and dials the last call that she had received on her phone a couple of minutes back.

She is breathing heavily. She somehow manages to speak, 'Wh . . . where . . .Where are you?'

The voice in her ears says, 'Behind you.'

Rupali immediately turns around. Just underneath the giant water storage tank, she sees the faint light of a mobile phone.

It's him! It's Arjun! Her Arjun!

He had come back. He wasn't lying when, moments back, he had woken her from her sleep and asked her to come to the rooftop.

Oh! My God! He wasn't lying . . . he is actually here for me! Rupali thinks to herself.

'Arjun!' she shouts his name.

She isn't scared any more. A part of her wants to rush to him. The other part is still trying to get a hold of her physical situation.

Arjun doesn't say anything. He has simply walked a few steps ahead into the faintly lit portion of the terrace and opens his arms. As he continues to stand there his eyes are stuck like glue to her. There is a sense of satisfaction in them; the satisfaction of seeing Rupali after so many hours.

Beep!! Beep!!

Rupali walks slowly towards him. And then she increases her pace, but stops just about two metres ahead of Arjun. Under the dim light of that yellow bulb installed over the water tank, she can see Arjun's face now. He is smiling.

'Arjun,' she calls his name again—this time with immense passion.

When, with a nod Arjun signals her to come into his arms, Rupali can't stop herself. She runs to cover that distance between them.

The shawl that she had been wearing has slipped down from her body. Instead, Arjun has wrapped her in his arms. Her head rests on his shoulder, while she locks her arms affectionately around him. Her eyes are closed. She doesn't want to see anything but just feel Arjun. He senses her quivering body. He rubs her back and tries to calm her down. Rupali believes that she won't be able to hold herself back. She is going to cry. It has been such a lovely surprise.

Beep!! Beep!!

'I am here! I am here!' Arjun whispers in her ears as he continues to offer her the much-needed warmth.

A tear rolls down her right eye and falls on Arjun's kurta. Her shaking body gradually calms down. She has tightened her grip around Arjun. With her ear over his chest, she realizes she can listen to his heartbeat. The smell of Arjun's body soaked in the fragrance of the cologne he is wearing mesmerizes her. She realizes that she is in a man's arms.

Beep!! Beep!!

No one says anything. There is no need to. Underneath an open dark sky on a silent cold rooftop, it is a magical experience for them. It is a beautiful moment. They want to live it to the fullest. They want to live it for long. The warmth of their bodies locked in an embrace comforts them in the cold.

Beep!! Beep!! Beep!! Beep!!

When Rupali finally opens her eyes, she sees over Arjun's shoulder a shadow against the horizon. The colour of the sky in that direction is transforming from black to red. It must be the east. The sun is about to rise. A brand new day is about to begin.

Beep!! Beep!! Beep!! Beep!! Beep!! Beep!!

Then, all of a sudden, Rupali wakes up to the horrible sound of the alarm set on her phone.

Eighteen

It must have been somewhere around 4 in the evening when he pulled down the stand of his bike.

Ahead of them was a vast piece of flatland, the periphery of which was marked by a barbwire, a few feet high, that ran from one vertical pole to another. Being a massive patch of unoccupied land, the place was a bit windy. It was a cloudy day and it felt as if it must have rained at a nearby place. The December air that was already cold, was moisture-laden as well.

As they took off their helmets, the cool breeze blew on their faces, refreshing them thoroughly. They rested their backs against the seat of the tilted bike.

Rupali felt nice. She closed her eyes and stretched her neck upwards to feel more of the breeze on her face. The air smelled of wet earth. Arjun looked into the mirror of his bike and ran his fingers through his hair ruffled by the helmet.

Behind the two of them, the traffic continued to zip past on the busy Delhi–Gurgaon National Highway no. 8. There were hundreds of cars and other vehicles on the road at any point of time. The combined noise of the engines of the running vehicles and that of their tyres pressing against the road, on the multi-lane highway was quite loud. It was a constant noise that had drowned every other sound in the vicinity.

Then there was a piercing whistle followed by a sound just like that of thundering clouds in the sky.

Even before turning back and looking at it, Rupali could make out what it was. Thrilled, she looked up immediately.

'Oh wow! There it is!' she said, pointing towards the sky.

It was an aircraft just above the highway, which was about to land and was flying towards her. Its rumble grew in a matter of seconds.

'Wow!' Rupali exclaimed joyfully. Her mouth was agape and it didn't close till the plane had come quite close to her. Then, within a split second, the plane flew right above her.

From that distance, even the wheels of the plane were clearly visible. Rupali could see the exact position of the flashing light on the wings. To observe that aerodynamic body, which appeared so big from so close, flying over her, was a treat to her eyes. Its noise levels began to go down.

'Did you see that?' she asked in sheer excitement. Her eyes followed the plane till it released a huge burst of air the moment its wheels touched the airstrip.

Watching the joy on her face, Arjun said, 'That was amazing!'

'Seriously, you liked it too?' Rupali asked excitedly. She thought it was too childish for someone like Arjun.

'Liked it? I loved it!' Arjun laughed. He was glad that he had been able to make Rupali happy.

'See, I told you naa . . .' Rupali said proudly and looked back at the airstrip where the plane was.

It was for the first time in the entire day that Rupali had enjoyed something beyond the thoughts of Arjun. Ever since she had woken up to that dream of being in his arms on the rooftop, she could sleep no further. Thoughts of Arjun did not let her sleep again. Even though it was just a dream, it had changed the entire meaning of her association with Arjun. It had shown her what till then she had been denying to herself.

She kept tossing and turning in bed, recalling that dream again and again. There was some sort of secret pleasure that she derived every time she recollected what she had seen. Step by step, slowly, everything in sequence, just the way it had happened in that dream. She had savoured every bit of it.

How sensuous it was for her to relive that embrace every time, for just one more time. Every time she did so, she felt Arjun's hands over her back. She wanted to touch herself exactly where Arjun had touched her. She imagined the masculine scent of his cologne and the smell of his body. She had taken a deep breath believing that she was inhaling it.

How she had wished to sleep again, hoping that the dream could proceed from where it had stopped. She had wanted to get hypnotized and let the drug of that dream completely take over her and transport her to a distant world, where the rooftop of her hostel block had become the best place to be. But then sleep had been miles away from her.

There had been moments when she was embarrassed about thinking that way. And when that had happened, she had pulled up her blanket over her head. She continued to have mixed feelings—sometimes she couldn't stop herself from thinking about it and sometimes she wanted to hide her thoughts from her own self.

'Have you ever sat in one of them?' Arjun asked, pointing to the plane that had just landed.

'Not yet,' Rupali replied and looked at Arjun. 'But someday I will. I have this dream of taking my family on a Euro trip,' she said and her eyes twinkled.

They were now talking about dreams; exactly what Rupali had suggested the other day over the phone—*I want to see planes landing and talk about our dreams*. 'How easily the two things had happened!' Arjun marvelled.

'You mean your husband and your kids!' Arjun asked. This time he wasn't looking at her but at the taxiing plane.

Rupali immediately responded, 'No, no. I meant my parents and my younger brother!' blushing shyly.

'Oh! So you plan to leave your husband and kids back and only fly your parents and brother?'

Rupali finally took the hint about what was cooking in Arjun's mind. She pretended to be angry.

'Arjun, why are you asking me all this?' she widened her eyes and gave him the look that meant—change the topic!

But Arjun was in no mood to let go. 'Oh, come on! Assuming you would get married in the future . . . so, then your family will also include your husband and your kids. Right Miss Rupali Sinha?' he asked.

'Hello! Mr Arjun Tyagi. I was talking about the near future. After I get a job for myself! Now will you change the topic?' she clarified but in a playfully aggressive tone.

Arjun enjoyed teasing her. But seeing her irritation, this time he let it go. 'Okay, okay. I got it. Relax now.'

After a few seconds, he thought of something and again asked, 'But in your not-so-near future, will you take your husband and kids on a holiday?'

'*Hey Bhagwaan!*' Rupali exclaimed, slapping her hand on her forehead. 'You are enjoying this. Aren't you?'

'Why are you dodging my question?' he accused.

'I am not!' Rupali reacted furiously.

'Then you are too shy to discuss that. *Hai na?*'

Rupali now kicked the ground with her foot. She could not decide what to say, so she turned back to face the airport with her arms across her chest, annoyed by this line of questioning.

Behind her, Arjun laughed. He was enjoying teasing her.

It was not that Rupali hated the conversation. She had clearly picked up the hint and she very well knew the possibilities of where that conversation could take them. Being a girl, she knew how guys make advances, when a light-hearted candid chat takes a turn towards more serious talk. But then so many thoughts were running in her mind that she felt irritated and confused.

She feared what would happen if what she had been thinking about Arjun's ultimate intentions was actually true. Even though she secretly wished Arjun would talk to her about his feelings for her, she felt she wasn't prepared to handle that conversation. Not at that moment.

On the other hand, she feared what would happen if she was completely wrong about Arjun's intentions behind initiating that discussion. *Will he say that? Does he even think about me in that way? It's I who dreamt about him and not he. But then for the past two days he has been messaging me endlessly.*

Doesn't that mean he has missed me, just the way I had missed him?

She thought of too many things at the same time. Her difficulty was that half of her thoughts were in contrast to the other half. But then, to her relief, no one could gauge what she was so absorbed in thinking about.

Another plane descended in the sky behind them. It bought Rupali some time to momentarily disconnect herself from the chaos of her mind. She looked back and up at the sky. She wanted to see the landing gear being deployed and the wheels coming out. But from where she could trace the plane, she was disappointed to find that it was already near landing.

The landing sequence was exactly the same as it was with the previous plane. And so were Rupali's actions of following the aircraft. Just that quite a bit of her excitement was missing this time. By the time the aircraft landed and was taxiing, Rupali had gone back to her previous thoughts.

After going over her thoughts again and again, she realized that it was going to be difficult for her to keep what she had been feeling about Arjun only to herself. Such thoughts were taking away her peace of mind. So she decided what she was going to do. She made up her mind to speak her heart out.

'Why would I take my husband on a holiday? Rather he should take me na,' she spoke.

She knew exactly which way the conversation would flow in a few minutes from there onwards. Yet she pretended as if she was just being honest. Maybe because pretending made things so much easier. It made her comfortable.

While she said so she was unable to hold back her smile;

she didn't look at Arjun but continued to focus on the taxiing plane. It kind of helped her. Even though her ears were tuned in on his response.

Seeing Rupali step into the conversation left Arjun amused. He hadn't sensed that coming—not after how she had reacted till a few minutes earlier. Her response became Arjun's cue to carry on that discussion. And when he heard what he had least expected from Rupali, in a state of overexcitement, he ended up doing something that he didn't want to do.

'Hmm . . . of course! That's what I would do!' he said and then realized his blunder!

What have I done! What would she think! he panicked. Then he tried to correct himself, 'I . . . I meant . . . in my case . . . my wife!'

Rupali was shocked and too embarrassed to acknowledge the first part of Arjun's answer. She pretended she hadn't heard it and responded naughtily, 'Okay, so where will YOU take YOUR wife on a holiday?'

Arjun was yet to recover from his blunder when Rupali dropped this other bomb over his head. And he conveniently fell into the new pit that Rupali had unknowingly dug for him. Unable to zero in on one holiday destination and caught in a strange feeling of imagining himself as a married man, he stammered, 'Where . . . wherever you want me to take . . . !'

That took the count of blunders to two; both in such a short span of time. And this guy was a youth leader!

Rupali froze, like a statue. She didn't even blink her eyes. She had never seen Arjun in such a state. Was he actually nervous now that she had turned the tables on him?

Arjun immediately jumped to rescue whatever was left of

his dignity. He stammered again, 'S . . . s . . . s . . . sorry! I . . . I . . . Okay . . . I . . . meant wherever she, I mean my . . . my . . . wife, would want to go. And if you could advise me on a good . . . a . . . a . . . yes a good holiday destination . . . then why not? That's what I meant. Yes! Exactly!'

Then he shut up.

His face had turned red. On a cold December evening, tiny drops of sweat appeared on his forehead. Suddenly, his body language lacked confidence. In a strange way he stole his eyes away from Rupali and looked here and there; at times at the airstrip and at times at the sky behind him, pretending he was waiting for another plane to land. When he could not decide what else he should say, he simply put his hand in the side pocket of his kurta and pulled out the keys of his bike. Then he kept fiddling with the keys. He looked so uncomfortable that Rupali was about to burst into laughter at any moment. However, she somehow managed to control herself.

After a short while of fidgeting around he looked at Rupali and said, 'Let's go now.'

Clad in his kurta–jeans and his favourite leather flip-flops was a second year student who had lead political movements and brought down systems in the past. Strange as it may sound, that day he had made a fool of himself in front of this first year girl—the same girl whom he had interrogated and scared the hell out of on her very first day on campus.

Till then he had known what he wanted to do that day. Till a few minutes back, in his mind he had planned it all—how he would stir the discussion, play with words and finally put Rupali in a spot, before he finally managed to say what was in his heart.

In his mind he had framed a step-by-step process to bell the cat. But then, when everything was going right, Rupali had hijacked the entire conversation. One wrong move and his plans went for a toss.

No matter how rough and tough Arjun had been in his life, when it came to matters of the heart, he was a novice. He would have glugged down half a dozen beer pints in two minutes, but words of love seldom rose from his throat. He was a man who was terrible at expressing his feelings. The last time he had gathered the courage to speak his heart out was when his mind was under the influence of alcohol.

'Arjun,' Rupali, who had so far been curiously observing Arjun's strange behaviour, finally spoke up. '*Aap please Charlie Chaplin ki tarah behave karna band karoge?*' (Will you please stop acting like Charlie Chaplin?)

Arjun obeyed and tried to calm down. The poor guy had things to tell and feelings to share. Yet he handed over the baton to Rupali and chose to keep quiet.

Sometimes the problem with silence is that the more it continues to prevail, the more awkward it becomes. And in such moments, the best way to go about it is to simply laugh at it. That's what Rupali did.

Understanding Arjun's state of mind and his recently shaken confidence, Rupali was the first one to laugh. Arjun knew that she was laughing at him. He felt an urge to join in her laughter, for that would mean facing up to the embarrassment. That way it's far easier to deal with embarrassment than to shy away from it. He laughed for the sheer fun of it. He laughed in order to let his inhibitions evaporate in that moment of fun.

Together they laughed for the fool Arjun had made of himself. And the more they thought about the whole episode, the more intense their laughter became. They were soon holding their stomachs and laughing.

Amidst their laughter, one more plane was on its way to land. The two of them could only acknowledge its arrival but unlike on the previous occasions, they didn't look up. They were not in a position to do so. When the plane flew over their heads, they were still holding their stomachs with bended knees. While looking at Rupali, Arjun pointed his finger towards the sky. Rupali waved and slowly they settled down.

'Oh boy! We laughed like two mad people. We even missed the landing!' Arjun said. Then grinning, he looked into Rupali's eyes and asked, 'Shall we leave now? It is getting . . .'

Rupali put a finger over her lips. 'Shh!' She then shook her head. 'No,' she said.

'But why?' inquired Arjun.

'I have yet to see the wheels coming down. Missed it both times,' she replied and then added, 'and moreover, we haven't completed our conversation on our dreams. Have we?'

'Well yes, we haven't done that yet . . . but,' Arjun accepted, '. . . but today seems like a bad day. I am making a fool of myself!'

'Bad day? But look around, it's such a beautiful evening!' Rupali pulled Arjun's leg.

'Yes, but I am mixing up things,' he argued back.

Rupali first smiled and then gracefully pointed out, 'That's because perhaps your mind and your heart are not in sync. We are talking about our dreams. Our dreams take birth in our hearts. Maybe you are not speaking your heart out, but only letting your mind do the talking. That's what is leading to chaos.'

Having said that, Rupali looked far away at the vast horizon that hung over the long airstrip. That changed the course and the depth of their discussion. They seemed very far away from the moment when they had been laughing crazily. The conversation took a grave turn.

'What you are saying is right. But the problem with dreams is that it sets expectations and it hurts when they are not met. Two and a half years back, I had dreamt of securing a commerce seat in this college. It never happened. And I am still fighting a battle to do away with reservations in DU. There are many such broken dreams . . .' Arjun was lot more serious now. Clearly, he had recovered from his previous nervousness.

'True. And equally true must be the fact that many other dreams would have come true in your life. The broader question is, when a few dreams do not come true, should we stop dreaming? And if that is true, one day everyone will stop dreaming because not all our dreams will come true. Instead, why not be optimistic and take encouragement from those that have come true and wish others will follow?' Rupali pointed out. For a moment she shifted her gaze back to Arjun and waited for him to reply.

Backed by Rupali's encouragement Arjun shared his view, 'Hmm . . . I agree. But certain dreams you can't fulfil on your own. You need someone else by your side to make those dreams come true.'

'Then what's stopping you from involving that someone? Reach out to that person and share your dreams . . .' she insisted.

'Of course! But then what if the other person's dream doesn't fit in with your dream?' Arjun questioned.

'If,' Rupali pointed out.

'Yes—if,' acknowledged Arjun, understanding that the probability of that unfavourable happening was only half.

'Then there are two possibilities. You persuade and convince the other person or you fail to do so. That means there is a 75 per cent chance of your dreams coming true.' She smiled after she'd wonderfully summed up everything into a probability outcome of a maths question.

Arjun rolled his eyes, appreciating Rupali's positivity and said, 'Okay *madam ji*. But are we going to talk only about my dreams? What about yours?'

Hearing that Rupali felt a bit dejected. Arjun was still trying to run away from sharing his feelings. All her attempts to encourage him to do so hadn't resulted in anything, it seemed. There was no point in beating around the bush now, Rupali realized. It was no longer exciting to play with words like husband, wife and holidays. It appeared senseless to her to talk about what would happen in their married lives when all she yearned for was to take the first step; to express her feelings; to experience a promising courtship period of her love life. The past hour's talks and her thoughts, which were a lot more streamlined and specific now, had given her enough confidence to speak for herself. She made up her mind. That was the moment and she was not going to play the game of ifs and buts any more.

She took a deep breath and began to speak slowly, as if she was reading something straight from her heart. And as if her heart was located somewhere on the western horizon of the sky where the sun was gradually setting.

'My dreams are quite simple, Arjun . . .' She paused for a moment and then continued, 'I want to do well in academics, secure a good future for myself and fulfil responsibilities that I have towards my family. I want to continue to stand up for things I believe in. I wish to see happiness around me. And while all this happens, I want to . . .' She stopped again, but only to resume after a second or two, '. . . I want to see you by my side. Arjun, I want to live the rest of my life with you.'

And then there was a silence between them as the words sunk in.

Even though the noise of the traffic persisted just as before, it was as if time had stopped and nothing moved. Even though another plane landed, neither Rupali nor Arjun looked at it. It was a moment that was about to change everything between them for rest of their lives.

Rupali turned her head and looked right at Arjun and finished whatever she had to say with her final line, 'That's what my dream is.'

Bliss had made its way into Arjun's eyes as he heard those final few words. Rupali had already successfully put to rest every bit of anxiety and panic in his heart. She had said it all so simply and with such ease! It had saved Arjun from the great difficulty of overcoming his fear of expressing his feelings to a girl. A deep sense of satisfaction came over Arjun's face. He was yet to speak and all this while he had been admiring the guts of the girl who stood in front of him. Who, only a few moments back, had proposed to him, something which the world expects to be a man's job. But isn't that why he admired Rupali—for her sheer courage to speak her heart; to call a spade a spade; to propose to a guy whom she believed she loved. That's what had always made her a special girl in Arjun's eyes.

It was going to take some time for the unimaginable amount of happiness to settle in. A few seconds or a couple of minutes were not going to be enough for him. For that matter, even a day's time was too less.

In the initial moments, the mere realization that it was all for real was hard to believe. Yes, it was for real and he wasn't drunk!

And so it was for Rupali. She wasn't dreaming again. Behind her calm and composed face there were hopes, there were fears and there were happy butterflies! It was a whole new world of experience for her. A moment she had never lived before. A moment she had never imagined would unfold this way.

'Can my dreams become a part of your dreams?' she politely asked, trying to catch Arjun's attention.

He wanted to say a hundred things, yet he struggled to say a single word. He searched for the right words that could describe what he was feeling at that very instant. When he found none, he simply nodded, grinning from ear to ear. His eyes could not hold back the immense happiness and had turned wet. He swallowed the lump in the back of his throat and when he felt he could talk he said, 'Your dreams are mine now!'

The two hearts erupted in joy. There was happiness in the air. A brand new chapter of Arjun and Rupali's life had just begun with Arjun's acceptance.

The gradually descending sun in the faraway horizon

made way for darkness. Rupali and Arjun barely had an idea of when exactly the sunlight dimmed and their vision became obscured. The otherwise dull-looking airstrip now glittered with blue, green, red and white lights that marked its boundaries. The airstrip had turned into a dance floor with colourful disco lights. The view looked picturesque as if when night falls the entire area gets an artistic makeover. As if the whole place was a nocturnal ecosystem that comes to life only when darkness falls. The well-lit buildings on the far left marked the airport hub that was not fully visible, yet one could easily make them out because of the light they were radiating. The only concrete structure clearly visible was the glass-bound air-traffic control room on a tower, the shape of which was like a giant high-rise water tank.

Behind them, the line of hotels on the Delhi–Gurgaon national highway, sparkled with their flashing billboards and running lights. Some of them changed colours at various intervals. The streetlights on the highway were turned on and so were the high-beam headlights on the racing vehicles.

Between these two spaces, amid the lighted darkness, was a new pair of lovebirds that continued to perch themselves on the motorbike and to savour the beauty of the moment. There was no one around them. They had the much-needed privacy. Arjun had moved his hand over Rupali's wrist and slid it down, making space for it in her palm. The touch was sensuous. It had triggered an adrenaline rush within Rupali. Yet she didn't pull her hand back. No one said anything. Rupali didn't even look at Arjun and let him do whatever was on his mind. She had partly surrendered herself. It wasn't just the touch of Arjun whom she had known for the past few months, it was also the touch of a man with whom she wanted to live the rest of her life.

Her heartbeat quickened. Arjun's forefinger made random circles inside her palm. It tickled her. He opened her fingers and then his fingers moved in between their gaps and held her hand tightly. It was a divine union. Arjun then raised their hands, still in each other's grip, close to his face. They were looking into each other's eyes—Arjun staring into hers. Rupali's heart sank when she could feel Arjun's breath falling on the back of her hand.

An aircraft flew over their heads, making a deafening noise. The wheels came down right above their heads; something that Rupali had waited to see for so long. But when it happened this time, Rupali was lost in living that moment when she felt Arjun's lips on the back of her hand and then of her fingers.

Rupali rested her head on Arjun's shoulder. The two of them watched a few more planes land. The array of open window shades, the well-lit interiors of the plane, along with the flashing wing and tail lights had made the airplane all the more spectacular. It was very exciting for them to see it land on a runway that was illuminated with stunning lights. At times, just before the plane made contact with the ground, the exhaust of heated air from the rear of the plane created a mirage-like effect, making the airstrip lights float, though only momentarily.

Hand in hand, Arjun and Rupali kept watching the spectacular view for a long time. They knew that this time would never come back. There is never a next time for the first proposal of anyone's life!

It is New Year's Eve. The girls from the hostel have had their way and managed to stay out till late in the night. A combination of emotional drama and gifts has worked to bribe the hostel gatekeepers. Outside, in the city, they are now celebrating New Year's Eve together.

But Rupali isn't with them. Far away from the hustle and bustle of the cheering city gearing up to welcome the New Year, she is taking a leisurely walk with Arjun behind the college block. This is an isolated street, one that leads to the trees that mark the dead end of the campus in the northern direction. Yet it's safe. During the semesters many boys and a few girls from their hostels come here to booze and fag. Being here has always meant being in the lap of nature. Only college students have had access to this zone. The beauty of this place is that it is never crowded, but then, at any time of the day, one can see a few faces relaxing in their own way.

But this evening is different. The semester break is on and there is no one here at this time of the night. The place is dead silent. As they walk, Arjun and Rupali get their much-needed privacy. To add to it is the layer of fog in the air that has dimmed the effect of the white streetlights glowing overhead. Visibility is limited to a few metres. It's like a white night. The sound of insects far away in the woods makes the place a bit spooky. Rupali moves as close to Arjun as possible to feel safer.

It's been a little more than twenty-four hours since she confessed her love to Arjun. After spending a very special night talking on *the phone and then spending a whole day together, this is the first moment of privacy bestowed to them by Mother Nature. They know that it's quite late for them to be here. But they find each other's company so addictive that they want to delay their goodbyes for as long as possible. They are not going to get such moments in isolation again. The vacations have come to an end. The college will reopen in a day's time and, from the following night, the hostel will be crammed again with students.*

Arjun has got something for her. He slides his hand into his pocket. Rupali anxiously waits for him to pull his hand out.

It's a pendant. A heart-shaped one.

Rupali's eyes glitter looking at it. 'For me?' she asks smiling.

Arjun nods.

'It's lovely,' she says while running her fingers over it after which she turns her back towards Arjun and lifts her hair from over the collar of her jacket.

Arjun accepts her invitation to clasp the pendant around her neck. When it's done, Rupali turns back towards him and looks at her pendant.

'This really looks nice! Thank you!' she says without looking at him. His eyes are glued to her new accessory.

Some time pass and they chose to take a walk.

So much has changed in our lives in this semester break,' Arjun says.

Rupali wonders how the days that she had thought would be the most difficult to pass, turned out to be the best time of her life on campus so far.

'I am glad I didn't go home for the vacations,' Rupali admitted.

They keep walking. It's colder towards the trees. The chill in the air makes Arjun long for Rupali's warmth. He wants to touch her; hold her in his arms. But he also wants to make sure that he doesn't end up scaring her. For a moment he debates with himself. He knows it is the perfect moment, one that may not come again soon. He doesn't want to waste it.

'It is fine, we are in love,' he assures himself and then cautiously makes his move. They have reached the end of the road and ahead of them are the wild bushes. They are about to turn back.

Rupali also wishes to get intimate. She rubs her hands and hints that she is feeling cold.

Two anxious hearts are getting ready to discover the next stage of their newly accepted relationship. Their excitement soon gives way to burning passion.

Right at that moment Rupali feels Arjun's hand over hers, trying to hold her. Right at that moment she stops. His touch is different tonight. She can feel it. It's the touch of a man who is craving to express his love in a manner that goes beyond words.

In that cold insulated night, she too wants to experience it. Without looking at him, she spreads apart her fingers, making way for his fingers to intertwine with hers. It's a sign for Arjun. All is okay. He begins to rub the back of her hand with his thumb.

His touch has accelerated her heartbeat. Instead of transforming warmth to her body, Arjun's physical touch has made her shiver. But then she doesn't want to leave his hand. She enjoys that moment. She wants to live that sensation of trembling in his arms.

Arjun reaches out for her other hand. Rupali surrenders herself. They are now facing each other. But she is too shy to look up at him. She is well aware of what's in his mind. Arjun loosens the grip of his hands and holds her face instead. He looks into her eyes. At that moment Rupali experiences an adrenaline rush. She can't face him and closes her eyes.

In the blurry depth of that cold white night, under the last streetlight on the abandoned stretch of the road that leads to the woods, he tries to look at Rupali's face—in the greatest possible detail. As if he is trying to remember the shape of her fine eyebrows and the slope of her eyelashes. As if he is trying to save a picture of her in his mind. From her chiselled nose his gaze slides down to her lips. He can make out the fragrance.

He tucks a few strands of her hair behind her right ear and prepares to say something. He is still holding her face between the palms of his hands.

'Rupali . . .' he says. His voice is husky.

She hears her name passionately called out by Arjun. But Rupali is in no position to respond. With her eyes still closed, she can make out Arjun's proximity to her. His breath on her face.

She sighs in that moment of bliss. Her lips part a bit.

Arjun is still staring at her face. '. . . Rupali . . . I love you. I so do.'

It's such bliss to listen to these words. She put her arms around him. His proximity has made her numb. The New Year is moments away. She is moments away from experiencing the first ever kiss of her life.

Gosh! This is happening. She knows she isn't dreaming. It is all for real. She is present in that moment. And she is prepared for it.

He bends down to kiss her. Arjun closes his eyes and their lips meet. There is an explosion of senses as Arjun goes deeper and sucks on her lower lip as if trying to extract all his share of love from her. He pulls her closer to himself. She tightens her arms around him and kisses him back with equal passion. They are now kissing each other hungrily as if they have waited for this all their lives. The cold, the darkness, the world around them ceases to matter. All they feel is each other—the wetness between their lips.

Their breathing gets heavier. Their kisses get deeper. And their sighs get louder. It's a divine moment for them.

They don't know how much time has passed. Suddenly, there is the noise of crackers around them. Up above the sheet of fog, the sky of Delhi is full of fireworks.

The magic of the moment is temporarily broken. They move apart a bit but still have their arms around each other.

'Happy new year!' Arjun says to a smiling Rupali, and goes back to kissing her.

Nineteen

After the vacations, life at DU began with a bang. Auto-rickshaws kept up the buzz by bustling in and out of the hostel campus—similar to how the scene had been more than two weeks ago. While a few students had returned to the campus on the night of 1 January, a majority of them had chosen to come back the next morning. A few, for whom attending classes on the first day after a vacation was the last thing on their mind, took the liberty of arriving only late in the afternoon.

Greetings and hugs were exchanged all day around the campus. Amidst a mass hostel room-dusting exercise, loud noises and screams intermittently erupted from various floors of the hostel blocks. When it came to backslapping and joking around, the girls' hostel was no different from the boys'.

Boxes of homemade sweets and other eatables were passed from room to room, from one hand to another, before they emptied up and made their way to the trash cans.

But the best of the stuff was always locked in trunks to be savoured later and only with best friends after locking the door—that was the unsaid rule.

Late in the evening, after the classes of the first day of the second semester got over, Rupali realized that everything had gone back to what it had been like before the vacation. From the day when the hostel had looked abandoned, with only a few girls left behind, to today, the difference was stark.

Every window on every floor of her hostel was lit once again. Sounds of music erupted in various rooms and floated in the corridors. The hostel mess was full again. No one who had gone on vacation had missed the hostel food. But once in the mess, they began to miss their home-cooked food.

However, the best part of the day for Rupali was when Saloni knocked at her door. The moment Rupali opened the door they celebrated their reunion with screams and hugs. It was Saloni who screamed louder. She continued to hold her roommate tightly, the two of them rocking in each other's arms like a swinging pendulum.

When they both came to rest, Saloni slightly pushed her best friend back to look at her. *'Kaisi hai tu, meri jaan?'* (How have you been, my darling?)

Rupali was extremely happy to finally get her roommate and best friend back. She had been waiting for her return since last evening. There was so much she had to share with her, for so much had happened in her life while Saloni was away.

'I'm fine, how was your trip?' Rupali asked.

Had Saloni not left the country and gone to Australia with her family for her vacations, she would have been up-to-date with Rupali's life. But then, had that happened, the two would not have looked forward to having a girly midnight-gossip session. 'Oh, it was so much fun! I will tell you what I did!' she smiled and winked.

Saloni then looked around at their room. Unlike other girls in the hostel, she had been spared the task of dusting and arranging her stuff. Rupali had taken care of it. She was the one who had kept the room neat and tidy.

They spent some time chit-chatting and randomly gossiping about things that were on top of Saloni's mind, after which Rupali suggested that she change her clothes so they could go and have their dinner. Saloni was not hungry at all, but she offered to give Rupali company. She opened her bag to pull out her T-shirt and pyjamas.

'Here! This is for you,' she said as she tossed a brown paper bag on Rupali's bed.

'What is it?' Rupali asked as she tore open the packet.

'Check it out yourself!' Saloni responded, busy trying to figure out where she had kept her own clothes inside her luggage.

'But there was no need to . . .' Rupali said, guessing it was a gift for her.

'Hello! Madam!' Saloni shouted back. 'I didn't spend my money on you! *Baap ke paison se liya hai.* This is all from my dad's money. So chill!'

'Why do you treat your father like that?' Rupali expressed concern and, as usual, Saloni didn't bother to answer her.

She then turned her attention to the bag and began pulling out the clothes inside it. There was a navy blue sweatshirt, a bottle of perfume and two pairs of lingerie—one red and one black.

Looking at the flimsy underwear Rupali exclaimed in shock, 'Haww! How could you get me this!' She was staring at a black lacy G-string. She felt shy even looking at it, so she immediately threw it back into the bag.

Watching her reaction, Saloni burst out laughing. She walked up to her and said, 'Come on! Isn't it sexy?', and pulled it out of the paper bag again. 'Why don't you try it on and show me?' she asked as she brandished it in front of Rupali.

'I call it lack of cloth!' Rupali said bluntly.

Saloni burst into a laugh again. 'No, stupid, these are in fashion. The ones that I've got for you are not available in India. *Ek to mein tere liye le ke aai.* Since I have got it especially for you, you will have to accept it.'

Rupali knew she was in trouble. Her roommate had not yet given up on her pledge to transform her into a modern Delhi girl. While she had been successful in moving her from salwar kameez to capris and sleeveless tops, and Rupali knew she wanted her to wear shorts, never in her wildest imagination had Rupali thought that her roommate would someday insist on what she should wear inside!

But she also knew that Saloni would not listen to her. She didn't want to offend her friend, as it was a gift she had bought for her. So she agreed to wear the G-string but on one condition—that there was no way she was going to try it in front of her; something Saloni was so comfortable doing openly in their room.

Rupali smiled. 'Okay, madam, you win! Now let's go for dinner or I'll go off to sleep!'

Post dinner, after a long leisurely walk in the cold night, during which they interacted with a few other girls from their batch, the roommates were back in their room. Saloni looked at her watch. It was almost midnight. She picked up her facewash kit and went to the washroom.

When she returned, she freaked out, *'It's damn cold!'* She complained about the cold water as soon as she came back to the room. She was shivering and quickly pulled out her towel and wiped her face and hands.

'Ha ha! Welcome back to Delhi from a warm Australia!' Rupali laughed. Everything in the room, too, was cold. Saloni thought about getting a room heater the very next day and, while saying so, she jumped into Rupali's bed and slipped inside her blanket. She placed her cold hands over Rupali's relatively warm ones.

'Ouch!' Rupali screamed.

'Mazaa aaya?' Saloni laughed, asking if Rupali had enjoyed her cold touch. She didn't wait for Rupali to react and asked, 'So tell me, what's going on?'

'What do you mean what's going on?' Rupali responded.

'What's the reason for this beautiful glow on your face, sweetheart?' she asked.

For a moment Rupali became very conscious, even though she had already planned to tell everything to Saloni.

'You are the reason. You have come back now, na!' Rupali reasoned.

Inside their blanket Saloni immediately tapped Rupali's hand and said, 'Give this bullshit to someone else, okay!' Saloni smiled with confidence. She had guessed it. Something was definitely going on!

'What?' Rupali attempted a weak defence.

'Achha! With whom were you exchanging SMSes while

I was talking to my basketball team friends outside the mess? Haan? Now tell me, what's going on!'

'Oh, come on! I was talking to my family,' Rupali lied. Saloni could make that out as Rupali avoided looking into her eyes.

'Really? Then let me check your cell . . .' saying that, Saloni stretched her arm over Rupali's body to reach out for her phone on the table.

'No. Please. No!' Rupali shouted and jumped at once to secure her phone.

There! She had said it all without saying anything!

With no iota of doubt in her mind, Saloni laughed slowly, '*Hey . . . hey . . . Betey! Sab samajh aa raha hai mujhe . . . hey . . . hey.*' She took her time to make use of the opportunity to see her roommate embarrassed at being caught red-handed.

And Rupali, who all this while had been waiting for the perfect opportunity to share what had happened in her life, never got a chance to do it the right way. She was all prepared to tell her roommate. But the way Saloni bluntly put things together and confronted Rupali, it made her change her mind. Unlike Saloni's nth crush, this was Rupali's first. And it was special. And she wanted to reveal it in the right way. But even before she could speak her heart, her roommate had guessed it and ridiculed her. Even though it was in a playful manner, it annoyed her.

When Rupali tried to speak again, she looked at Saloni, who mischievously kept raising her eyebrows, waiting for her to speak up. Her hesitation had stopped her from speaking.

Saloni began grinning. 'Come on! Tell me what all

happened with you in my absence. I can smell love!' she said, winking.

Rupali blushed. 'Okay,' she said.

Suddenly, Saloni jumped out of the bed, switched off the lights, jumped back in, grabbed a pillow to place between her legs and said, 'Yes! Now tell me, quickly!'

Twenty

With the start of the second semester, campus politics became the priority again. There had been a case of violence reported in which a few students from the students' union in power had clashed with another group of students. The fight had erupted due to the alleged harassment of a girl outside the campus by someone who was an active member of the students' union. Two of the boys from the other group were reportedly admitted to the ICU. When the police had booked a few members of the students' union, the rest of the union had called a strike in a few colleges asking the vice-chancellor to intervene and get them out. Even though majority of the students were not in favour of it, they all were silenced. Rumours also alleged that a nexus of drug traffickers was flourishing in the university and that they had the backing of the members of the students' union. This brought to light questions about how the union was spending its funds. A demand was also raised to bring in more transparency in this.

It appeared that the party that had come to power had long forgotten the promises it had made in its manifesto before the elections. Within the students' union itself there were differences over how a few representatives had begun to act selfishly to further their political ambitions. Drunk on power and full of arrogance, they had dreams of joining active state and central politics as soon as they stepped out of university. Unwillingness to share accountability had led to blame games. Everyone passed the buck.

The prime reason behind the mess in the students' union was the absence of its godfather, Mahajan—the accounts professor who was now behind bars. He was the one who had the strongest influence on the union, thereby maintaining a fine balance between all the stakeholders. The elected representatives used to fear him and, therefore, obey him. They looked up to him to get the necessary approvals from higher authorities wherever his influence was required. He was their liaison between the campus and national politics. Not that under Mahajan's watch illicit things never happened. They did prevail, but then he had brought a method to the madness. In Mahajan's absence, a few members in the union fought among themselves to retain power. And when that happened, the rift was out in the open.

Slowly, the union began to fall apart. The youth wing in-charge of the parent party at the Delhi state and national level, too, felt the heat. Mahajan's absence had created a void between them. If the status quo persisted, it would be impossible for the party to win the next DU elections that were supposed to commence after the next batch arrived. With one semester left in hand, the students' union badly needed to repair itself and deliver on its promises.

But this was also the time when other parties were planning to get the students' support and raise their voices against the menace of the party in power.

'So what are we going to do now?' Prosonjeet asked.

This was a Sunday morning meeting when the key party members had assembled on the rooftop of the college block. It was a casual meeting that had been called to kick-start the planning of the party strategy for that semester. Having lost an election in the current season, the members were eyeing to do things in a different way and looking at the next season's election.

'We need to bring awareness. Let's remind people about what was promised to them and what has been delivered. Worse, how drunk on the power of authority, the current students' union is running the political game as if it is it's monopoly. We will involve students from various colleges and faculties and ask questions to the union,' Arjun pointed out.

A key member, who in the previous season had fought the election for the post of president and lost, had expressed his wish to opt out of fighting it yet again. There were murmurs among the members that Arjun should fill in that gap and fight the election for the post of president. His maturity to handle things and take decisions had earned him the party's confidence. Till the previous year, he had been a strong volunteer for their party.

'And how do we do that?' someone in the gathering asked.

'We will leverage the power of social media,' Rupali pitched in.

Rupali's meteoric rise to fame in the previous semester in the whole of DU for her courage and her selfless determination to do what's right had catapulted her into students' politics. In the course of time, she learnt that in order to bring a change, it was important to step in and become a part of the system. Her six months in DU made her realize this. She realized the importance of politics and the results it can deliver if the right people step in. This is how someone who abhorred the idea of politics became pro politics. When Arjun and other members of his party invited her to join them, she happily accepted the invitation. But she was clear that she was not going to fight the elections. She wanted to use the platform to fulfil her social responsibilities. So she was there in the party now.

She continued, 'Mahajan went to jail primarily because the video of his shameful act went viral. It had triggered the sentiments of the masses in a way that we couldn't ever have imagined. It had made the students raise their voices on social forums, something they feared to do in the open. We all are present on various online forums. If we can use these online social circles beyond the boundaries of networking for fun and channelize them to run our campaigns we will be able to achieve a lot!'

This plan was different from the stereotypical speeches, pamphlets and banners mode of election preparation. Rupali's focus was to push the digital and social mode of strategy-making. People acknowledged Rupali's point of view. Most of them agreed, while a few had their reservations, on which Arjun wanted to hold a healthy debate. They did a quick analysis of the strengths and weaknesses of the power of online social media campaigns. It turned out that the pros were lot more than the cons. Everyone was of the view that because they had an entire semester's time in hand, they must at least experiment with the idea. Arjun invited Madhab to help them come up with a rough idea of what could possibly be done. Taking a cue from Madhab's suggestions the team brainstormed. From making a Facebook page in the name of their party to making real-time videos about the grass-root problems in DU and uploading them on YouTube, there were various such options at hand. The more they ideated, the more possibilities they saw.

Before the members dispersed, roles and responsibilities were distributed. From generic thoughts, they wanted to arrive at specific bullet-point actions. People undertook the task of doing more research on their specific areas of action before they planned to meet again during the same week.

After the meeting ended, Rupali had plans to pay a visit to Arjun's mother. The previous day, when she had expressed her urge to eat home-cooked food, Arjun had asked her to visit his home. 'You can meet Ma as well. In fact, we can have lunch together.'

Rupali had double-checked that Arjun had really meant it, after which she had happily agreed. It didn't make her feel concerned that she was going to meet the mother of the guy whom she was now in a relationship with! Arjun, too, made it sound casual. In the past, he had invited various friends, including girls, to his place and they had eaten food cooked by his mother. It was quite regular for him. On one occasion even Raheema, who treated Arjun like her brother, had visited his place.

Rupali sat beside Arjun in his jeep. Madhab and Prosonjeet jumped on to the back seat. They had asked Arjun to drop them at the nearest metro station. The two of them had plans to watch a matinee show. They had insisted Arjun and Rupali to join them, but Rupali excused herself saying that she would prefer home-cooked food to a movie.

'You will drop me back at the hostel, right?' she asked Arjun as soon as he started the engine.

'Yes,' Arjun said, looking at her.

'Will it take us more than an hour to reach your home?'

'Traffic on Sunday is quite less. We should not take more than forty minutes,' Arjun replied.

'And what time will you drop me back?' Rupali again questioned.

This time she heard Madhab and Prosonjeet giggling behind them. She turned back to ask them what was the matter. They first denied that they had been giggling, but could not hold their laughter when they looked at each other.

'What?' Rupali asked out of curiosity. She could make out that they were hiding something from her. So she looked at Arjun, hoping that he would help her understand what she had missed.

'Six months back when they had been sitting on the back seat of this jeep, they had seen me interrogating you. Today they are seeing you interrogate me! And that's why these idiots are enjoying!' Arjun said focusing on the road ahead of him.

That statement immediately took Rupali to the past. For the first time she realized that about six months back, in her first week of college, the two guys who had sat on that seat in that very jeep, when she had been planting the sapling, were Prosonjeet and Madhab. And all she had remembered was the bearded face of Arjun.

Twenty-one

Sometime later, after having dropped off the two friends, Arjun parked the vehicle near the entrance of his house. Rupali was eager to meet his mother. She stepped out of the jeep, and unlocked the main gate and walked in.

'Hey! Wait for me to come! Guess this is my house!' Arjun yelled from behind her.

Rupali immediately stopped. She turned back and smiled. Then she waited at the porch for Arjun to join her.

The entrance door was open. Arjun stepped inside and called for his mother. Rupali followed him inside the drawing-cum-dining room. It was neat and tidy. It had everything a middle-class drawing room comprised of. A sofa set on one end and a dining table on the other, curtains on the windows and showpieces on the shelves of a glass cupboard.

'Come,' Arjun asked Rupali to follow him.

Arjun escorted her to a bedroom where his mother sat on the bed busy cutting vegetables and watching a soap on television.

'Namaste aunty,' Rupali greeted her and touched her feet.

'*Arey bas bas . . . Jiti raho beta!*' Arjun's mother blessed her.

For the next few minutes Arjun was quiet, watching the two ladies interact and get to know each other. They talked and soon his mother was asking Rupali all sorts of questions, about her family, home town etc., which Rupali answered patiently.

Arjun's mother didn't forget to mention and praise Rupali's courage in the Mahajan case about which she had come to know about a few months back from her son. Rupali felt happy that she had remembered. Arjun too was happily surprised.

The television was still on in the background. Arjun picked up the remote and pressed the mute button. That suddenly turned everyone's attention to what was playing on the screen. Rupali noted that even her mother watches that particular serial which Arjun's mother had been watching. This made her talk about a few more TV serials and she happily recalled the names she had heard from her mother.

Arjun got up and was about to walk out of the room when his mother asked where he was going.

'I need to get some party banners made, Ma. You two have a good time,' he said and left.

His mother shouted and asked when he would return, to which he shouted his reply from the main gate—he would come back in an hour or so.

Once Arjun had left, his mother clasped her hand to her forehead and expressed her disappointment when she said, 'All the time the only thing he is bothered about is his party work. Sometimes I can't understand whether he joined college to study or to become a politician!'

Rupali smiled as she listened to a mother's innocent

concerns. She thought Rupali too was worried about Arjun, like her. But she realized she was wrong when she heard what Rupali had to say, 'Aunty, today the country, like never before, needs politicians like your son. Arjun is doing the right thing.'

For Arjun's mother, it wasn't new to listen to Arjun's friends praising him for the choices he had made in his life. Time and again, various friends and party volunteers who had visited the house in the past, had talked about Arjun's ability and his honesty in the arena of campus politics.

But then she was a mother who hadn't kept up pace with the changing times. In her mind, she still perceived politicians to be shrewd and involved in every sort of antisocial activity. How could she forget the terrible days when none of the political leaders had turned up to see her ailing husband who had been so loyal to his party?

Arjun's absence had given more space for her to open up to Rupali. She had always had these close discussions with Arjun's friends whenever they visited her. She always felt that Arjun kept things to himself. So she never missed an opportunity to know about a different side of Arjun from his friends.

Looking at the picture of Arjun's father that hung on the wall towards her left, she mentioned how he once used to work as an active volunteer in a state-level party. She told Rupali that her husband was a man of great ideologies and that he had played an active role in extending the reach of the party among the lower-class colonies and slums of Delhi. He would rarely ask for party money and would often spend his own savings for party work. She said that in order to campaign for his party he had given his sweat and blood, so much so that he was once caned by the Delhi police and later booked in the lock-up for protesting against the corrupt administration in power. 'Political prisoner,' she said.

But then, when times changed and the party he worked for came into power, things too changed along with it. Now it was time for the leaders of his party to fulfil their own interests. That was also the time when Arjun's father discovered that he was suffering from cancer. Even when he was dying, no leader visited him. They were busy counting the money they had been making. It was only his friends and acquaintances who knew him for the man he was, who visited him. Better treatment in a better hospital could have saved him. But they didn't have the money as a good portion of what Arjun's father had earned, he had already spent on party work. He believed his party too was his family. But unfortunately, the leaders of the party never shared that feeling.

'*Phir kya mila is politics se humey?*' His mother asked disappointedly about what they had possibly gained from politics. 'Nothing,' she said, looking at the garlanded photograph of him.

Ever since then Arjun's mother had lost faith in politicians. That was a long time back. Her wounds had healed to a large extent. But now, seeing her son get into politics, it seemed to her that he had not learnt from his father's mistakes.

But that's exactly what Rupali's point was. She felt that because there was a dire need to clean politics of such people, it was essential that good people stepped into the dirty puddle of politics.

'If good people don't step in, the people of this country will have no option but to choose the bad representatives as their leaders and hand over their fates to them,' she felt. Rupali reached out to Arjun's mother and held her hands. 'Just because something awful has happened in the past doesn't mean the future too would be like that.'

The warm touch of her hands, that affectionate gesture and that positivity in her thoughts gave solace to Arjun's mother. She wanted to believe in Rupali's words but she didn't say anything.

'Now let me give you a hand with this,' Rupali said, picking up the plate of vegetables that Arjun's mother had been cutting from. And despite protests from Arjun's mother, Rupali succeeded in taking over the knife to chop the vegetables. A little later, Rupali helped Arjun's mother with the cooking. She was impressed to see Rupali's expertise with kitchen chores. None of Arjun's friends, including girls who had visited her earlier, knew anything about cooking. The only time they had entered the kitchen was to keep their used dishes after having eaten their meal. Rupali's interests and abilities were in stark contrast to theirs.

Rupali's presence in the kitchen made Arjun's mother recall her own daughter, who would also help her with the cooking. She mentioned her to Rupali and talked about dishes she used to make. 'What nice kheer she used to make!' she recalled.

But this time Rupali didn't let her turn sad by remembering her daughter. She knew what had happened to her. Arjun had mentioned about her when the two of them had been to the Bangla Sahib gurudwara.

'Next time, I will make it for you!' she announced and hugged her. Arjun's mother hugged her back and smiled. With that, Rupali smartly changed the course of their discussion.

As the two of them cooked the food together, they talked about a lot of other things. At times Arjun's mother talked about Arjun's childhood and how naughty he used to be then. At times, Rupali talked about her family back at her native place.

Half an hour later, when Arjun came back, the three of them ate their lunch at the dining table. Rupali and Arjun sat opposite each other. From the way Arjun's mother spoke about Rupali and her cooking skills, Arjun realized that Rupali had impressed her. Arjun winked naughtily at Rupali, who blushed.

He was about to have his first bite when his mother asked him how they'd met.

Both Rupali and Arjun looked at each other and laughed. Arjun's mother was now more than curious to know what was so funny about what she had asked. Rupali took the opportunity to tell her all that had happened on her first day in college. Listening to her, Arjun's mother playfully slapped Arjun's shoulder and said, 'Stop scaring the girls at least!'

'*Arey*, she's not among those who get scared! She has instead scared big shots!' Arjun laughed and began eating.

Late in the afternoon, Rupali and Arjun stood at the gate. Arjun's mother came from inside to see Rupali off. Rupali folded her hands in respect and Arjun's mother ran her hand over her head. She blessed her and asked her to visit her again and, if possible, soon. 'You are a nice girl. *Meri beti ki yaad dila di tuney*,' (You remind me of my daughter) she said.

Rupali warmly hugged Arjun's mother, who continued to pat her head.

When Arjun started the engine of his jeep, the two ladies separated. Rupali waved at Arjun's mother and sat next to Arjun. He reversed the jeep and they left the house.

'So how was it?' Arjun asked once they were on their way back.

'The food?' Rupali asked, deliberately trying to tease him.

'Huh? Food? No! Meeting my mom!'

'Hmm . . . *thik tha*!' (It was okay!) Rupali said without enthusiasm.

Arjun immediately applied the brakes of his jeep and looked angrily at Rupali.

'Okay, okay, baba. Relax. I was kidding!' Rupali replied. 'It was great to meet your mom. She's a lovely person—so simple, so loving. I thoroughly enjoyed her company and being in your house today!'

'You are telling the truth this time. Right?' Arjun asked. His face was shining due to the praise.

Rupali nodded.

A little smile replaced the temporary fake anger on Arjun's face. He resumed driving. For quite some time, Rupali talked about her discussion with his mom with a lot of joy. Arjun felt nice. It was a good idea to invite Rupali to meet his mother.

By the time they were close to the campus, the course of the discussion drifted to campus politics and the party's campaign that they were going to kick-start. It happened when Rupali asked Arjun whether he had been able to accomplish the work for which he had gone out before lunch. Arjun said that it would take some time before they got the banners.

'There is something I want to talk about, Arjun,' Rupali said. 'We won't win the election,' she said bluntly.

It bothered him when Rupali said that.

'What! What are you saying?'

'See, I don't have any experience in campus politics. But from what I see, you and your group have differences with other student bodies on campus. I have been thinking about this . . .'

'What differences? With whom?' Arjun interrupted. He was a little worked up by what he considered as Rupali's negative thoughts, even before she had spent a week working in the party.

Rupali put her hand on Arjun's and asked him to calm down. She politely explained her point to Arjun. Rupali pointed out how on the one hand they wanted to campaign and win the trust of the students, but on the other, they were disconnected from various student bodies.

When Arjun asked if she was talking about other political outfits in the university, she said no.

'Then?' asked Arjun.

'Your differences with the music club. Your stand against students who got admission through the reservation and quota system,' Rupali answered.

'There is no way we are going to shake hands with them to win the elections!'

'*But Arjun aap meri baat ko samajh hi nahi rahe ho!*' she said, trying to explain her point. 'I am an active member of the music club. None of our members hates you or your party. I mean our party.' She immediately corrected herself. 'Rather, a majority of them hate the party in power right now, for they ditched the music club last year and played opportunistic politics by telling the students in DU that the club supported them.

'Trust me on this, Arjun. The music club would still want to remain apolitical. However, the club wants to contribute to a change in the university. I realized that it too has common goals like that of our party. The music club is the most important wing of DU's entire cultural club that also includes theatre groups. If we work with them, there is a lot we can achieve!

'Am I making any sense? Are you still angry?' Rupali quickly checked before explaining further.

'Hmm . . . go on,' Arjun nodded.

'Great. So, I was saying that there is a lot that is common between the cultural club and DU. The music club wants to undo the image that they secretly supported the current student union. Tenzing, who leads our club, also represents our college at the DU level. He is fighting a battle on behalf of the entire North-east student community which DU still doesn't consider as an inclusive part. They are looked upon as if they are not one among us. It is an important issue and if we, as a political outfit, make DU a level playing field for students from every ethnicity, and include this issue in our agenda, we will be able to grab the support of the entire student body from the North-east. The theatre groups have always taken up these burning issues in their street plays and dramas. Abolishing the reservation system and awarding seats only on merit has been the message of various members of this group. This is exactly what you have been fighting for. This is why you joined student politics in the first place. Demanding that reservation be abolished means inviting the wrath of those who got admitted only on the basis of the quota system and they certainly won't vote for you. They will resist and endorse other political outfits which are in favour of reservation.'

Listening to Rupali's thoughts, Arjun didn't realize when he had slowed the pace of his jeep. Rupali's points were important. The way Rupali had connected the dots made a lot of sense. He could see that Rupali's idea was to get the support of smaller independent bodies that were apolitical in nature and, therefore, could become mouthpieces of their party's ideas. In an academic environment creative groups play an important role in spreading the message. That's exactly what Rupali had pointed at.

'And just because they are not affiliated to any particular party, people would be more open to understanding a neutral point of view and then synthesize their decision about whom to vote for,' she said in the end.

By the time the two of them arrived at the hostel, Arjun was game to discuss Rupali's point of view with the others in the party. He had already begun analysing the pros and cons of the discussed approach. Working on removing differences was definitely not going to be an overnight task. It needed mutual trust and respect. Rupali was his biggest hope in bridging the gap between his party and her music club. That day, Arjun again felt grateful that he had Rupali in his life and now in his mission.

Just when Rupali was about to get off the jeep, Arjun

asked her for Tenzing's number. Rupali smiled and searched for it in her phonebook. Arjun pulled his phone out of his pocket to take the number when he saw an unread message. It was from his mother—a rare thing, for she always preferred calling Arjun rather than texting him. To add to his thrill, it was in English, a language she wasn't quite comfortable in.

He blushed on reading it and told Rupali that there was something his mom had texted him. 'You hit the bullseye in the first meeting,' he said and couldn't stop smiling.

'What is it?' Rupali asked excitedly.

Arjun read the message his mother had sent: 'I like your this friend. What about you?'

Twenty-two

'Did the sun rise from the west today?'

They were pulling his leg.

Arjun's new avatar had instantly become the talking point the moment he drove into the north campus in the morning. They had all gathered at their daily spot at Shafi's teashop to wish Arjun on his birthday. Raheema too was a part of the gathering. She hadn't forgotten Arjun's birthday and knew where to find him. So on her way to the campus in the morning she stopped at Shafi's teashop and was amused to find a brand-new version of Arjun, though she had taken a few seconds to identify him.

When the people surrounding Arjun asked Raheema her opinion on Arjun's new look she was at first in two minds. She said that he certainly looked different.

Someone in the crowd shouted, 'Raheema didi, don't be diplomatic. Tell the truth!'

'*Kya na banu, bhaiya?*' Raheema inquired, wondering what she should not 'be', unable to understand the meaning of 'diplomatic'.

'He is certainly looking different today. That we all know.

But tell us whether he is looking good or bad!'

Raheema understood this time and spent one full minute analysing Arjun's new look. Then she finally started shaking her head and a smile came on her face. She said, *'Clean shave karke is T-shirt mein zabardast lag rahe hain. Ekdum hero maafik.'* (Clean shaven and in a T-shirt! He is looking as dashing as a hero!)

Everyone laughed, clapped and cheered at that.

But the show was not over. In the next ten minutes the group had asked almost every passer-by they knew to vote on Arjun's changed looks. Being the birthday boy, Arjun could not do much about becoming the object of their fun. This was the standard practice on campus and the rumour that he had sacrificed his beard and kurta for the sake of his girlfriend added fuel to the fire.

As per their little survey, six out of nine people had voted in favour of Arjun's new look. The survey included Raheema, Shafi, two of Shafi's helpers, a rickshaw-puller, two lecturers and two girls from the college basketball team who were there after playing a morning game.

Shafi was one among the three who believed his clean-shaven look took away the macho factor he possessed. The rickshaw-puller who was a regular at the teashop, agreed. One reason to approve of the bearded look was that they both had beards themselves and they felt cheated, as if Arjun had left their clan. One of Shafi's helpers followed his employers' opinion.

However, since it was Arjun's birthday, and Shafi was a man with a big heart, he announced that the tea was on him that day. He also offered the group the new cookies that his distributor had supplied him the night before.

Meanwhile, back in her room, Rupali had received the news of her boyfriend's makeover. Saloni, who too was there along with the other basketball players, had secretly clicked Arjun's picture and messaged it to her roommate. She had called him her lover in her message: '*Tera majnu*'.

Rupali was overjoyed to see that Arjun had kept his promise. A day before, over the phone she had insisted that she would like to see Arjun clean shaven and in an attire that is anything but a kurta. She wanted the birthday boy to look different and special than his usual self. To her surprise, Arjun had agreed. But in return he had demanded that she too wear something of his choice. Rupali agreed, but her agreement was based on Arjun's fulfilment of his promise first. She liked how he looked on her cellphone and was excited about seeing him with her own eyes. However, as she was yet to finish her pre-reads and complete her pending assignment, she had to contain her excitement.

It was later in the day, during the break, that she finally got to see him. It was at the party meeting that had been called at the college rooftop to discuss the social media campaign they had talked about a few days back.

Rupali was all smiles the moment she spotted Arjun among the party members. Her arrival made everyone turn around, including Arjun, who stopped in the middle of what he had been discussing. She could not help but blush as she walked towards him.

'Ladies and gentlemen, meet the lady behind this man Arjun 2.0!' Prosonjeet announced. Everyone laughed. Some clapped as well.

Even though it was an awkward moment for him, Arjun

was waiting for Rupali's reaction, unaware that she had already seen his picture. Rupali laughed and joined in with the group. When she stopped right in front of Arjun, she complimented him, saying, '*Aap achey lag rahey ho.*' (You are looking nice.) She knew people would tease her. But by then, the party members had become like family to her. She didn't mind facing the whistles, the hooting and the cheers. She knew she had to be honest and appreciative of what her guy had done for her.

'Guys, Arjun passed the test!' Madhab shouted.

'But Rupali, how did you get this out of him?' Prosonjeet asked.

'He asked me to fulfil one of his requests. I agreed on the condition that he first fulfil my request. His request was so dear to him, that he agreed to accept mine!' Rupali answered.

'And now YOU have to keep YOUR promise,' Arjun reminded her.

Rupali nodded.

'That's nice, Rupali. There are a couple of things I want Arjun to do. Maybe I will get in touch with you offline. You can put them as your next requests,' Prosonjeet mocked.

'*Saaley kaminey,*' Arjun light-heartedly flung out his hand and gripped Prosonjeet's neck.

Trying to release himself out of Arjun's grip, Prosonjeet shouted, 'Guys let's do it now or I'm going to die!'

In no time, someone grabbed his legs and lifted Arjun up. Someone else grabbed his arms and some others lifted him from the back. It happened so quickly that Rupali and two other girls in that gathering barely got a chance to pull themselves out of the circle.

For the next couple of minutes, Rupali watched Arjun's body being tossed up in the air as he got his birthday bumps. They began counting. Arjun screamed, he yelled, he abused. But it all got drowned in the mad screams of his friends. His body swung up and down in the air, again and again and again till they counted to twenty-one. Rupali felt pity for Arjun, but could not do much about it. Only in the end, when the bumpy stretch of the birthday celebrations was over, did she inquire, 'Are you all right?'

The innocent concern was bound to be taken lightly as everyone laughed.

'All right folks, shall we now get down to the work for which we had all gathered here? I mean, apart from giving me birthday bumps,' Arjun reminded everyone. The next fifteen minutes, in contrast to the previous ones, involved serious discussions that were packed with questions and answers. The party members brought in their findings and laid out a draft of an action plan. Rupali made bullet points of the important items and wrote them on the last pages of her notebook. Together they decided the name of the Facebook page that they were going to create and what the profile would look like. Someone had already created a Gmail ID in the name of their party. The plan was to use the same ID everywhere, including a YouTube video that they were supposed to create. They discussed the nature of the content and the frequency with which they were going to update posts. The technicalities of how they were going to expand and reach out to the entire DU, college by college, were also covered. For the day, the main agenda was a video that Madhab wanted to shoot in the evening. He had called everyone to meet outside the college on the campus lawns. 'If everything goes right, we will upload this video by next Sunday,' he had said.

It was little over break time, when they all called off the meeting and dispersed to attend their respective classes. Just before leaving, Rupali reminded Arjun that they had planned to meet Tenzing as well. Arjun confirmed the time. He wanted to finish the conversation before Madhab's video shoot. Rupali confirmed the venue. Music room it was.

~

'What bothers me the most is this word—chinki. That day when your party members disrupted our set-up, this is what they called me. No matter what I do, as an individual I don't have an identity. None of us from the North-east has an individual identity. We are just chinki. All of us,' Tenzing said, his voice full of pain and despair.

Arjun and Rupali who sat on a table in front of Tenzing, heard him as he continued to speak.

'This is a serious mindset issue that stretches beyond the walls of DU. You know how much more difficult it is for one of us to find a house on rent in this city, just because of our appearance? Looking at our eyes and our hairstyle, some call us Chinese. This really hurts. We are as much Indian as you are!' he said, pointing to both of them.

After a moment's silence, when Arjun had absorbed all that Tenzing had spoken, he said, 'I understand what you are saying. And I agree that this is a mindset issue. Perhaps for a long time the rest of India was never bothered enough to even consider this as an issue, forget addressing it.'

'Yeah . . .' Rupali began. Both Arjun and Tenzing looked at her. '. . . And even if this issue extends beyond the walls of this university, it must be addressed at least in the university. Maybe then we can take the solution to the world beyond DU as well. At the least we must practise inclusivity of every ethnicity on our campuses,' she said.

'But you know what?' she added, 'Instead of finding a solution, I am wondering how it came into existence in the first place. I mean to say, why is it that we tend to sideline the North-east and detach the people from this geography? As if they are not a part of us?'

Tenzing shrugged, 'Glad to see someone is at least bothering to think about it! You know, during the last semester break a good number of us had discussed this. A group of us were on the same train till Kolkata, after which we were supposed to change trains to our native states in the North-east. Here's what we felt. You see it all starts at the school level. While our history books cover everything that happened in this country from Jammu and Kashmir to Tamil Nadu, they rarely talk about a detailed history of the North-eastern states. People never get to know about us when they are introduced to the rest of India. Our history is simply missing in those books. Therein lies the neglect. The perception that we aren't as important as the other states of this country.

'The geographical knowledge of us Indians is so skewed that we will know the capital of Punjab, but won't know the capital of Mizoram. Forget the capitals, a majority doesn't even know the names of the North-eastern states. I don't live in a hostel. Two years back, before I moved into my rented apartment, when I told my landlord that I am from the North-east, he asked me which country that was in! This is the reality; such a huge lack of awareness. There are seven sister states in the North-east, besides the Himalayan state of Sikkim. How many times have you seen a face from the North-east on the cover of a magazine representing a common Indian or, for that matter, doing a TV commercial? How many actresses are there in Bollywood from this part of the country? Hollywood has accepted Chinese actors, but in our own country Bollywood is yet to take people from the North-east into consideration. People believe that we are distinguished from the rest of the Indians because of our looks and our accent. But if you think deeper, that's not true. Because had it been about looks, a Sikh with his turban and his beard, is far more distinguishable than me. In this country, where language and accent change every fifty kilometres, how does it matter what my accent is?

'People discriminate against us because they are not familiar with us. They are familiar with the culture of a Punjabi and a Tamilian but aren't that familiar with ours. And some would also argue, rightly so, that why cluster our states as North-east? Why not remember our states with their own names? But to arrive at that level, the country should first know about us. The sad truth is that we are for sure legal citizens of India, but unfortunately, we are not accepted as cultural citizens of India,' Tenzing sighed.

His words echoed in Arjun's ears. He was stunned to understand the gravity of the issue. Every word he had said was an eye-opener for Rupali. It definitely influenced the way she looked at the issue. The in-depth insights that Tenzing had provided and, especially, the way he had delivered that little speech had left Arjun thinking. The impact of it was such that Arjun requested Tenzing to consider his invitation to hold an interactive session with the rest of his party members at the next meeting. He also insisted on inviting a few of his friends from the North-east.

'I can do so, but not in the capacity of a music club member, but as a student from the North-east who is fighting for our identity in DU,' Tenzing said.

'Yes. I understand that,' Arjun replied.

Even after that intense meeting, the interactions of that long day were not yet over for Rupali and Arjun. They had to meet again on the campus lawns for Madhab's shoot. But before that, Rupali had to fulfil the wish Arjun had made.

~

As decided, they had all gathered on the college lawns. In walked a young girl in a stunning white lacey sleeveless top and brown leggings. Her hair had been blow-dried to fall in soft curls around her face and from under the big black sunglasses you could only see a soft mouth with pink gloss. She was wearing long silver earrings and brown high-heeled shoes. She walked slowly towards them.

Instantly, all eyes were on her. When the boys in the group saw this glamorous young woman walking towards them, they began to wonder who she was.

Only when Rupali joined them and took off her sunglasses, did their jaws drop.

'I don't believe this!' Madhab said.

'Yeah . . . we don't either . . .' murmured others with eyes and mouths wide open in disbelief.

Arjun stared at her and then walked closer—his eyes looking at her admiringly. It was clear that he wasn't able to say anything.

'My goodness, Rupali! You look hot!' Shipra, one of the party members, complimented.

'What are you guys up to? Giving us surprises! First Arjun appeared like a different person and now you in this glam avatar?' Prosonjeet said loudly.

'I had to keep my promise!' Rupali smiled seductively and looked at Arjun, who still seemed shocked.

'But your transformation is far bigger than that of Arjun's. Straight from the . . . uh, sorry, but *behenji* type . . . to a Delhi girl. What do you say, guys?' Prosonjeet shouted.

There was a loud cheer all around them. A lot of hooting and whistling. Rupali smiled shyly as she stood next to Arjun, who was now beaming, looking quite proud of his girlfriend. She received a lot of compliments on how she was able to carry off the western look. Rupali secretly thanked Saloni for this. Had it not been for her, she wouldn't have been able to put this look together.

Meanwhile, Arjun kept happily staring at her. He couldn't take his eyes off her in that body-hugging, figure-revealing, top. Through the strappy neckline he could see her chiselled neck and collarbones. He gazed at the smooth skin and the delicacy of her shoulders that were otherwise always hidden behind the suits that she wore. He didn't forget to notice that Rupali was still wearing the pendant that he had gifted her on New Year's Eve. She never took it off.

He wanted to touch her, feel her skin. He wanted to hold her, kiss her, soak in the heady aroma of her perfume. He wondered how a girl, whom he had till then admired for being a mature intelligent person with a good heart, could also have such a sensual side to her! And how powerful was his attraction to her. Arjun tried to control his thoughts but couldn't. Rupali had ignited something else in his heart.

Suddenly, Madhab shouted and brought Arjun out of his daze. He wanted to shoot in natural light before the evening got darker. It was a *nukkad naatak,* a street play, that he had thought about and wanted to capture on his handycam. The scene was that of a guy and a girl in love who had just got admitted to the same college in DU. He chose three couples from his team. Rupali and Arjun became his final choice for their real-life love story. He explained the first scene to everyone. The couple was supposed to lie down on the lawn and look into each other's eyes as they talked about how they visualized spending the next few years of their lives in college. In the next portion of the video he wanted to showcase the contrast between their dreams and the ground reality. However, today was about the first part. The second part he had planned to shoot on another day, in another setting.

Madhab asked everyone to take their positions and perform the act together. He said they should keep talking normally while he walked a full circle with his camera to capture the scene. Everyone, including those who were going to act, was excited.

Most couples wondered what they would talk about. Only Rupali and Arjun weren't too bothered about it. Madhab had given them all a few lines. He was not going to record the voices that evening. There was a voice-over he planned to do while editing the video.

'Thank you for keeping your promise,' Arjun whispered as he looked into Rupali's eyes.

Rupali smiled.

They were lying on the slightly prickly grass of the lawns. The gentle sunlight was streaming through the clouds and on their bright faces. Rupali's pendant intermittently flashed the falling sunlight and playfully blinded Arjun's eyes.

'Gosh! You look beautiful!'

Rupali glowed with happiness. Finally, her Arjun had said what she wanted to hear. She found it difficult to continue looking into his eyes. She knew it was a different moment, different from the times they had met before. She knew that Arjun was looking at her in a way that he had never done before. Secretly, she wanted him to notice more of her and not her clothes.

Suddenly, she realized Madhab was saying something. He had been shouting at Arjun initially and when the lost-in-his-girlfriend-guy didn't hear him for the third time, Madhab called out Rupali's name. She heard it the second time.

'Thank you so much, Rupali, for finally listening to me. What are you guys up to?' Madhab shouted. The others continued to make fun of Arjun who had completely missed the point.

When Arjun turned and looked at Madhab, the latter asked him, 'You are lost, my friend! What are you up to? Please turn towards your left and be aware that I am here!'

'Alright! Alright! Here we are trying to give you a realistic shot and you are shouting at us!' Arjun said, following his instructions. He was taking the whole thing quite lightly.

'Yes, this is fine now. Look at Rupali and continue talking,' Madhab shouted, looking at the screen of his handycam.

Madhab continued to shoot them for the next few minutes. After the entire shoot was done and while reviewing his recording he looked at Arjun and Rupali and said, 'You guys have an amazing chemistry!'

'No! Hold me like this. Yes. This way. Perfect!'

It's the third and final night of the college annual fest. The lawns outside the administrative block bustle with students enjoying and cheering a live band of Bollywood singers. About half an hour back, the college's music club had received a phenomenal response when Tenzing and Rupali had sung a peppy number 'Masti ki Paatshaala'—a song that had unofficially become DU's anthem. Even though the original number didn't have a female singer, Tenzing's idea of experimenting with a female voice had worked brilliantly. It was the final number and they had dedicated it to the students and life at DU in general. The boys and girls in the audience had loved it and they showed their enthusiasm for it by clapping their hands in the air, in sync with the rhythm of the song. Since almost everyone knew the catchy lyrics, the crowd sang along. It was fun and they ended the song to loud cheers of, 'Once more!'

But that was half an hour back. Now that the star attraction of the night, the Bollywood band, had begun its show, she slipped out of the gathering to enjoy Arjun's company. Evenings like these, ones full of festivities, enhances the feeling of being in love and makes it even more joyful. Along with the celebrations with friends, giving them the slip to catch a few private moments with that special someone makes the experience delightfully adventurous.

From behind her, Arjun slips his hands around Rupali's waist, just the way she suggested a second back. He interlocks them around her naval. She is wearing a white V-neck cardigan over a white-collared top. A pair of blue denims complete the look. That's her music club's dress code for the night's performance.

'Aren't you afraid that someone might turn up here and see us?' Arjun gently asks as he rests his chin over her shoulder.

They are looking down at the gathering that is enjoying the live band.

'No,' she says and turns her head to face him.

From the rooftop, the view of the ground is electrifying and spectacular.

'Are you?' she asks, wondering if he is scared that someone might see them.

The music, the songs and the thumping of the crowd continues in the background of what looks like a relaxed conversation.

A smile erupts at the corner of his lips and takes sufficient time to flourish further. He shakes his head to brush away Rupali's concern and then kisses her forehead. She looks into his eyes. She trusts him and turns her head back to the gathering five levels below them.

No one speaks for a while. They are enjoying the music. They are enjoying being together in that moment.

'It's a beautiful night. Isn't it?' Rupali says.

'Yes, it is,' Arjun replies in a half whisper. He kisses her neck while he speaks, it tickles her and she giggles. Then he nuzzles her neck and he can feel her suddenly tense up. They are so close . . .

He looks up at the sky to distract himself.

'What happened?' Rupali asks. She can sense that he has moved away a bit.

He takes a moment and then softly says, 'Winters are bidding goodbye. You noticed?' Strangely, he sounds sad when he says so.

Rupali smiles, 'Yes they are.'

Arjun doesn't say anything and rests his chin back on her shoulder. In response, she puts her hand on his cheek and pats it affectionately. 'And you don't want them to end?'

Arjun knows that it doesn't matter what he wishes for and that seasons will change when their time comes. Yet half-heartedly he says, 'I wish they wouldn't . . .' and then adds, 'But how does it matter?'

Rupali smiles at his response. She turns her head for the second time, this time to look at Arjun's unhappy face. Her hand is still over his cheek.

'It matters to me,' she says, holding out a smile. 'But why don't you want them to end?'

Arjun takes another moment to frame his thoughts. 'These winters are special. Our love story began with them.' He says and slips his hands in between her cardigan and her top. Then he sighs and Rupali can feel his breath behind her ear. It makes her feel warm. She runs her hands over her cardigan to feel Arjun's hand inside it.

'True, these winters are special and I will never forget them,' she slowly begins. 'But Arjun, just like these winters, I want to see and enjoy other seasons with you. I look forward to them.'

'Hmm. You're right again,' Arjun says. Suddenly he's looking at things differently—just like she showed him to. He realizes that he isn't sad about the ebbing winters any more. And just like Rupali, he too is looking forward to the spring that's about to surround their love.

Twenty-three

It was Abbaas Hanif, an MLA from the ruling party in Delhi, who moved Mahajan's bail plea. Mahajan's aunt, a distant relative, had passed away in a remote village near the Delhi–Haryana border. Using his political muscle and through the able services of his advocate, Hanif had filed a plea that Mahajan should get bail to grieve the loss of his dear aunt.

In many ways Hanif was Mahajan's godfather. Under his nose and with his blessings, Mahajan had gained power and flourished in DU. In return, Mahajan worked for Hanif and focused on building and empowering the youth wing of the party. But that was a few months back, before Mahajan was caught in a disgraceful act and was locked in jail. Back then, other politicians had broken all contact with Mahajan because being seen with a tainted professor would be inviting trouble. Hanif had told him to have patience.

'Let the dust settle and I will do something for your escape,' he had said.

Hanif kept his word, more so because he needed Mahajan. He needed him to revive the dying students' union. He needed him because, besides Mahajan, there was no one to control the functions of the union. He had traded his escape to bring things to an order in DU politics for Hanif. Hanif knew that in Mahajan's absence, his party's youth wing was on the verge of collapse. And this meant trouble for Hanif's party. As Indian politics was moving towards wooing the youth of this country, losing their hold in DU was not something they could afford at that time. Not limiting it to a bail of two weeks, Hanif had planned to keep Mahajan out of the prison for a longer time on the fake grounds of ill-health.

This certainly was opportunistic politics, but then there was no other way for Hanif and Mahajan. With the second semester due to end in just two months and the approaching final exams, they had little time left in their hands. Mahajan knew that if he didn't act fast, he would not be of any use to the party he was loyal to. Then, he would be back in the jail. He, therefore, had no other option but to deliver results to Hanif at any cost.

Out of the jail, he assessed the ground realities and the students' inclination towards the political parties. He also gauged the teacher association's mindset on campus politics. He didn't need to visit the campus for his little research. His trustworthy sources reached his house on getting the first call from him. The situation was grim, he analysed. The fact that there was not much time left in their hands, made matters worse.

Amidst all this, Arjun's party was gaining a strong momentum in the entire university. In the past three months their campaign, based on issues like the anti-quota movement, inclusivity of students of all ethnicity—with a special focus on North-eastern students, betterment of hostels and the life of students on campus, had got the support of numerous students' groups. The online social networking campaign had played a major role in this movement. More than 50,000 students in DU, across various colleges, had joined their Facebook page. One of the reasons behind gaining a huge number of followers in such a short time was their crowd-sourced online events that had gone viral. It was Rupali's idea to host a tab on their page where people could report what they saw as a problem on their campus. It started as a fun activity with photographs of stray dogs having sex in the courtyard of their hostel being uploaded, but soon became an important forum. From unhygienic kitchen areas in messes, to poor Wi-Fi signal in the hostel floors, everything made its way to this page. People not only wrote about their problems, they also clicked and posted pictures as proof. While the party volunteers commented on the valid problems and included them in their agenda, the page also invited the interests of the Einsteins and Newtons of DU. They offered low-cost yet good-quality solutions to problems mentioned by other students. Time and again they reminded the students that, if the party comes to power, they should be given the first chance to fix the problems they had brought under the scanner. They asked for an opportunity to prove their mettle.

Such was the influence of this Facebook page that even the students' union in power had started picking up on problems highlighted on the page and tried to fix them. However, they only focused on the really small issues to gain brownie points.

The page became so famous that it also grabbed the attention of the alumni of DU. This led to a new idea among the party workers—connecting with alumni and holding alumni–gyan sessions closer to the placement season.

Not only did Rupali bridge the gap between the cultural club and the party, she also brought in fresh faces to join the party; many of them were girls from her batch. She felt that their party's gender ratio was completely skewed in favour of the boys and that there wasn't enough representation from the girls. With her positive image, the party managed to register more than 35 per cent of girls as active members. Initially, the older party volunteers were bothered to see so many first year students joining them. They had raised the point that the lack of experience in campus politics that the first year batch would bring would dilute the party's core team. To that, Rupali pointed out that lack of prior experience would also mean that their vision would not be clouded by the baggage of past politics.

'Fresh minds will bring fresh ideas with them,' she had said.

Despite all the good work she had done, Rupali never got carried away. She was clear from the first day that she didn't want to stand for any post in the elections, even though many of her party workers suggested her name as a candidate. Her motto was clear. She wanted to work for a party that promised to make DU a better place to live in and study.

'But what about our core issue, the fight against the reservation system?' Madhab questioned.

The party members had gathered to refine the points on their agenda.

'I understand that reservation is a problematic area in our admission process,' Rupali replied to Madhab and to everyone who had gathered.

A few volunteers were already in favour of what Rupali was saying.

'Then why are you not giving it the due importance?' a voice in the gathering asked.

'Because I feel the issue also has room for a healthy discussion. On our Facebook page, a number of sportspersons from this university have written about why we should not be anti-sports quota while we fight to abolish other quotas and promote meritocracy,' she reasoned.

'I have been saying the same thing for the past two years,' Prosonjeet added.

'Are we now diluting our stand on this subject? Support some quotas and reject others? That's hypocrisy, no?' Madhab said. A few voices supported him.

'It's not like that, Madhab,' Prosonjeet argued.

'Then why are you vouching for sports quota?' Madhab asked back.

This time Rupali intervened to answer. She had already thought through all that she had to say. She began to speak in a composed manner.

'Okay, so here are my thoughts. And as I said, we should hold a healthy debate on this and then follow what the majority believes in,' she said. 'Guys, we all need to understand why, as a party, we are against reservation. Because meritorious students miss out, right? Plus, there is the menace of students making fake OBC/ST/SC certificates to get backdoor entry, thanks to the corruption in our country.

'In twenty-first-century India, should we continue to get privileges for taking birth in a particular caste and category? Doesn't this whole system work against real merit? We all agree that it does and that is why we all are fighting against it. And our stand is that, for anything, the HRD ministry should abolish such quotas and rather endorse a category for economically backward students and sponsor their education. But here again, the admission should be based on merit. Students should not be differentiated on the basis of their caste but on their economical background—whether or not their parents are in a position to support their education. A poor student from a general category should deserve a sponsorship and not a wealthy SC student. But unlike other quotas, the sports quota retains the value of merit. This isn't a quota that awards your fate of taking birth in a particular caste or sect of the society; it rightfully awards your ability to prove that you are better than others in the field of sports. You are not bestowed this privilege by birth, but you have to earn it. And this makes it a level playing field for all of us.

'As a nation, other than the religion of cricket, we are so sports-deficient that in spite of a population of more than a billion people we only grab two to three medals in the Olympics. We need to support the initiatives to endorse sports and credit marks for it. In our fight to abolish the inept quota system, let's not throw the baby out with the bath water.'

~

'The real threat isn't Arjun and his seasoned party members,' Mahajan said as he finished consuming the last sip of his tea in Hanif's drawing room.

Hanif had called him to get a status update on the campus politics and see what needed to be done in the little time they had in their hand.

'What do you mean? If they are not the real threat, who is it then? As per my sources, those students are going to stand for elections. Isn't this true?' Hanif asked in surprise.

'Yes, your information is right. But those senior students aren't the real threat—it is that first year girl,' Mahajan revealed in a bitter and vengeful tone. His eyes narrowed in anger as he recalled his interaction with her. In fact, Mahajan brought Rupali into the conversation to serve two purposes—nipping the revolution of abolishing the quota system in the bud and punishing the girl who had put him in this position in the first place.

'A girl from the first year?' Hanif asked as he opened the box of paan placed on the table in front of him.

'The one with whom I have some unfinished business!' Mahajan said. His eyes were glued to the surface of the glass table in front of him.

'Oh, you mean the same girl who got you . . .' he stopped his sentence midway. He was very pleased—if there was another motive other than just politics, it was even better.

Mahajan turned his head to look at Hanif. Hanif could see a mix of pain and anger in his eyes. 'Yes. That same girl.'

'Hmm . . .'

'She has united a few key student groups in DU with her party. They now have a vast support base. And I believe she isn't done. They will reach out to the remaining student bodies also in the coming days.'

'What sort of student groups and bodies are you talking about, Mahajan?'

'The music club, the theatre groups, for that matter, the entire cultural group, and not just at the college level. Things have now moved beyond a particular college. They are getting support from the entire university. The creative groups, through their events and shows, can become the voice of the party. They have a huge impact on their audience's mind, even though they aren't a part of the party. Not only this, my sources have updated me that she has got a lot of female students to enrol in their campaign. DU girls, so far, were not very interested in elections and voting. They are trying to sell the dream of more girl power in DU!' Mahajan said, almost spitting the words out.

'Damn! Mahajan. This way we will be routed in DU. Don't we have any students' group on our side who are willing to support us?' Hanif asked placing a paan inside his mouth.

'There is one. It's not an official group, but an unofficial one constituting the boys and girls who got admitted under various quotas. That includes the ones whom we helped get in through the back door. Arjun's party is against the quota system. Clearly, they won't be voting for them. Picking up from Arjun's party, now other parties are also protesting against the reservation system. So they will definitely vote for us,' Mahajan explained.

Hanif took a few moments to absorb all that Mahajan had said. He then tried to think of all the probable ways to save the sinking ship of his party in DU. Later in the day he was supposed to meet the student union leaders and chalk out a strategy for the elections. But, for Mahajan, his right-hand man in DU, he had some sensitive and difficult tasks in his mind.

'Then it's clear what you should do. Polarize the atmosphere. Create tension between quota students and others. Instil fear in the minds of the students in the reservation category about what will happen if DU loses the quota system. Anyhow, in DU elections, only about 40 per cent of the entire student strength votes. The remaining 60 per cent isn't bothered about elections. If we can get 95 per cent of the reservation-category students to come out and vote on election day, we will still have a chance. With no other party in favour of the quota, they will vote for us. But to push them to vote, you need to orchestrate a battle between them. Sell them the idea of fighting for their rights. And in this battle, if an OBC student is hurt and gets admitted in an ICU, it will only fuel the fire. The media will run a story—*Dalit boy brutally attacked in DU*. That will get our party the brownie points. You know what I mean?'

'Of course!' Mahajan nodded. He knew that in this short span of time only a sensational gimmick could work in their favour.

As Mahajan racked his brains to break the bigger task into various smaller tasks, Hanif slid back in his comfortable chair and enjoyed his paan. As he savoured the flavour of it, he patiently waited for Mahajan to ask him questions in case he had any. But Mahajan was crystal clear in his understanding.

The next time Hanif opened his paan-stained mouth to speak, he asked Mahajan, 'But I am more worried about this first year girl . . . whatever her name is. How is she managing to get the support of all these groups?'

'She is too smart for her age. At the cost of my image, the bitch has built her own. She won't fight the elections. But she has cunningly trapped the party's presidential candidate in the web of her love. That's her level of smartness!'

'Oh, so that guy Arjun and this girl . . .' Hanif raised his hand in the air and moved his finger as if trying to connect the dots, when Mahajan nodded his head and said, *'Janaab, ishq aur raajniti saath saath chal rahey hain.'* (Sir, love and politics are moving hand in hand.)

Then they both became thoughtful.

Suddenly, Hanif broke his silence. What he said next was going to change everything in Arjun's life.

'If a first year girl can control such senior boys, if she can send a cunning professor like you behind bars, just imagine Mahajan, what she will be capable of when she lands in third year . . .' He paused for a while to give Mahajan time to think. Then he slowly spoke, '. . . *Saanp ko jitni jaldi kuchal do badhiya hai.'* (The sooner you kill off the snake, the better it is.)

~

By then, with Saloni's help, Rupali had also roped in Saloni's boyfriend Imran, who was a key player in the college basketball team, to their party folds. That was the beginning of various sports' clubs supporting Arjun's party.

'And I want to kiss you there, under your ear, behind your earring . . .'

Her eyes are closed. Without letting him know, she touches herself behind her left ear. She is mildly trembling. In response to his sensuous voice, her voice now gets softer.

'Then?'

'Then I want to inhale your fragrance from your neck to the depression below your collarbone . . .'

'Umm! But, I am . . . I am . . . not wearing any deodorant right now.'

'I said, I want to smell you. Your body. Not the deodorant.'

'Ahh!'

She runs her finger over her collarbone and wonders how her body smells. There is silence from her end.

He gets worried. 'Are you fine? Are you . . .'

'And then?' she interrupts.

'Hmm . . . And then I am going to tickle your collarbone with my tongue!'

'Ouch! Ha . . . Ha . . .'

'You are enjoying this, aren't you?'

'And then?'

She doesn't want to have a conversation.

'Well, on my way my tongue gets distracted and moves to your bra strap. I have to run my tongue above it. I am going to lick it.'

She sighs, intoxicated with pleasure.

'But I am . . . I am . . . not wearing anything that has a strap.'

'So what are you wearing, then?'

'Only a T-shirt. Nothing with a strap.'

'Just a T-shirt?'

'No! I mean . . . Yes! A T-shirt and shorts.'

'Well then, I will pull the T-shirt down your shoulder.'

She pulls it down. Her shoulder is bare.

She takes a second to catch her breath. The pitch of her voice gets weaker again.

'Then?'

'I slip my other hand under your top and hold your waist.'

'Oh God!' she whispers.

'. . . My fingers crawl up the arch of your slender waist and move towards your stomach.'

Her other hand is busy holding the phone, so she leaves the stretched neck of her T-shirt and reaches out for her waistline. She runs her fingers in sync with Arjun's words.

'And then?'

'I can see your navel now.'

'Oh!' she gasps.

A few seconds pass and no one speaks. The silence itself has turned sensual with possibilities.

'Aren't you going to say "and then"?'

A moment passes. She is trying to absorb it all. Meanwhile, a debate has erupted between her heart and her mind. Should she draw a line? And, if so, when?

Her heart wins the battle.

'And then?' she asks softly.

His heart beats faster.

'I want to kiss you there, Rupali. In the depths of your navel. I want to run my tongue inside the moist skin of your belly button. God! I so want to do it right now . . .'

Her fingers automatically crawl down to her navel. They trace a sensuous circle around it and her forefinger slips into the depression of her belly button. She continues to listen to Arjun who is still saying something.

'. . . I want to blow a warm puff of breath into it. And I want to blow it far above your stomach.'

With her finger she draws an imaginary line above her navel. The moment her fingers meet the baseline of her top, her eyes open. Arjun is still continuing to talk.

This time her mind wins the battle.

'Alright. Stop!'

She catches her breath and takes a moment to calm down.

'What happened?'

A couple of seconds pass.

'I can't just . . . I . . .'

'Are you embarrassed? Did I embarrass you?'

'No, you didn't. I am not embarrassed. But I guess I am shy.'

Again a moment of silence passes between them.

'Hmm . . . it's fine.'

'I am sorry, Arjun.'

'Hey! It's okay. Relax.'

'You hate me. Don't you?'

'I love you.'

His words bring her comfort. She is feeling lighter and more open about it.

'But I loved all that you were doing, even though it was all in my imagination. Just like magic.'

'Well then, why did you stop me in the middle?'

'Hmm . . . I don't know. Maybe because as much as I enjoyed the imagination part of it, I was also conscious of your presence, even though you are only on the phone. I mean . . . I . . . don't know exactly. I guess . . . I guess, I enjoyed the virtual you, but then the fact that the real you was able to listen to me and that I was reacting to your voice . . . sort of interfered with my thoughts. Am I making any sense?'

'Wow! That's so complex. But anyway . . .' he laughed.

'Listen, I don't want to sound like a hypocrite. I accept that I enjoyed it. But then . . .'

'Ha ha. Chill, girl! I know you aren't a hypocrite. So stop justifying yourself.'

'Hmm . . . Maybe I will need some time to open up.'

'So shall I call you in half an hour?'

'Arjun!'

'Okay. Okay. Relax.'

After talking for a while she hangs up the call. She turns in her bed and looks at the table clock. It's 6.30 a.m. There is still some time before she has to get up. She then stares at the vacant bed on Saloni's side. She had left for her parents' house the night before to attend a get-together. She thinks about how her roommate's absence has allowed her a private romantic moment with Arjun.

Then she begins to recall her conversation with Arjun. The way her Arjun was in the process of sketching his desires on the canvas of her body. Exactly in the same sequence. She closes her eyes and touches herself again. She imagines Arjun by her side, and in her bed. She imagines him sliding her T-shirt up. She imagines her hand to be Arjun's hand. She imagines Arjun seeing her body.

And this time, she doesn't stop in the middle.

Twenty-four

When dusk fell, the roads of north campus dipped into darkness that was then bravely battled by the glowing yellow streetlights. There was an unusual breeze blowing. It appeared that at any moment it could take the shape of a dust storm. The sky was cloudy, but not cloudy enough to forebode rain.

Outside her college campus, Rupali walked alone on one of the roads that led to where Arjun was supposed to pick her up from. He was supposed to take her to his home for an early dinner that he himself had cooked for her. Except for a few students she crossed on the way, the road was quite empty.

Wanting to look her best and on Arjun's request, she wore the salwar suit that she had worn on her first day to college—a pink kurti with white churidar. She had rarely worn the set and even ten months later it looked as if it was brand new. Rupali wore a pair of new silver earrings, the glitter from which sparkled on her cheeks. Her sandals were white, matching her dupatta which time and again caught the gentle breeze. As she waited for Arjun, her excitement building up within her, she raised her wrist and sniffed it. Saloni had lent

Rupali her perfume and every time she smelled it, she felt happy and thankful about it.

'Try it, babes. It will hypnotize your man!' Saloni had said.

Rupali smiled as she recalled those words. She smelled nice.

Just then, from behind her, a fast-moving van abruptly came to a screeching halt right beside her. The door slid open. Two men jumped out of it, grabbed Rupali by her arms and pulled her into the car. The doors of the van closed just as quickly. The driver accelerated the vehicle and for a brief moment, the tyres rotated extremely fast and threw up some dirt from the road. Then, in a flash, the van sped away from that stretch of the road.

It all happened in the blink of an eye, giving absolutely no time to Rupali to even react. Even before she could shout, even before she could retaliate or understand what was happening, Rupali was inside the moving van with all its doors locked.

On the dimly lit street, a few students checked with each other if what they had just seen had actually happened.

Rupali's first reaction was to scream. She screamed her heart out. Simultaneously, she tried to reach out for the handle of the sliding door of the van—but in vain. She was not strong or quick enough. The guy on her left immediately overpowered her and pulled her back. Rupali struggled again, but could not move her hands by even an inch. Instead, the same guy pushed her arms behind her back and tied them with a rope. Rupali screamed even louder and, gathering all her strength, she tried to lift her body and push herself away from them. But caught in between two guys she had nowhere to go. All she could do was keep struggling and screaming.

She tried to look for people on the road. She wondered if her shouts would grab someone's attention—anyone's attention. But the windows of the van were tinted and the van was swerving from one side to another, so it seemed very unlikely.

With her heart pounding, Rupali looked around her. Besides the two guys on the back seat, two more men sat in front. One of them was the driver. Rupali could not see their faces clearly, but she was sure that she hadn't seen any of them before. However, from their shabby clothes, body language and little bit of conversation, they appeared to be local goons.

The moment her brain registered what had just happened with her, and understood the horror of the situation, she panicked. Her breathing became heavy. In an effort to calm herself down she took stock of the situation she was in. She was bleeding from her right ankle that had got hurt when the two men had pulled her inside. Her feet had been dragged against the edge of the van. The strap of her right sandal had torn off. Her arms, where the men had dug their fingers to lift her up, hurt terribly. There were specks of dirt on her white dupatta, which was now haphazardly stretched across her neck.

'Babloo iske purse mein se mobile nikal ke switch off kar pehle. Fir muh band kar saali ka!' (Search her purse for her mobile and switch it off first. Then shut her damn mouth!) the guy on the seat next to the driver shouted.

His command was immediately followed. The guy on the left quickly searched her purse, switched off her mobile and took all the cash he could find. He then threw it behind the seat. Rupali could only watch as the other guy had his hand pressed on her mouth. The tight grip he had on her face and the stink of his dirty hand nearly made her choke. Rupali continued to struggle but she was fast losing this battle of strength.

The van was now speeding on a straight road. It seemed like it was heading out of the city. The guy next to the driver was giving the directions. At one point he called someone up from his mobile and updated the person about his location as well as the status of things.

When all her energy had drained out, Rupali closed her eyes. Noticing that she'd stopped struggling, the guy who was holding her loosened his grip. With that, Rupali's thoughts became clearer. She began to wonder who these people were and what they wanted from her.

She used the opportunity the loose grip provided her and asked in a panting broken voice, *'Kaun hain aap log?'* (Who are you?)

No one replied. So she repeated her question.

'Yeh jaanna tere liye zaroori nahi hai,' (That's none of your business) the other guy on the back seat announced angrily.

Rupali became restless. She reached out to the guys on the front seat and pleaded, 'But why have you picked me up? You could have been mistaken!'

Hearing that, the guy next to the driver turned around. He switched on the overhead light in the vehicle to show his face, 'It's you who had made the mistake of messing with Mahajan,' he said coldly and showed her his mobile on which he had her photograph.

A chill ran down Rupali's spine. *So she really had been kidnapped by these goons!*

She stared at the man—he had a long bearded face with

large eyes that almost popped out of his head. A huge red *tika* ran down his wheatish forehead. He had long hair and wore an earring in his right ear. His eyes were bloodshot and his breath had the pungent smell of cheap alcohol. He stared back at Rupali and grinned, scaring the hell out of her. He then raised his hand and passed on a quarter bottle of alcohol to his companions at the back. Then he switched off the light.

Rupali's breath was caught in her throat as she sat scared shit.

'Wha . . . wha . . . What are you . . . huh . . . huh . . . going to do?' she stammered. Then she began to sob loudly, 'Please, I beg you, let me go . . . please . . .'

'Shut up,' said the man in front. They ignored her pleading and continued to drink.

Taking advantage of their momentary lack of attention, Rupali bit at the wrist of the guy who had his arms around her body. The guy screamed in pain. Rupali didn't release his hand till he loosened his hold. Then she threw herself over the other man in an attempt to reach for the windowpane.

It appeared as if she had gained some energy in the past few minutes and that now she was utilizing it to the fullest possible extent. She hit her forehead against the window, attempting to break the glass. She shouted hard, praying that someone outside would hear her.

The other guy tried to pull her back. He held her by the neck. Rupali resisted and shrieked her lungs out. She kicked and shoved the other guy. Every limb, every muscle of her body moved in protest.

But unfortunately, Rupali's struggle didn't last for too long. All of it led to nothing. Her screams were buried under the volume of the music that the driver in the front had increased. Outside those tinted glasses, the road stretched and stretched—there was no one around on that dead cold night.

Another scream escaped from her throat before she collapsed into tears. She was scared and shaking. What could she do now? Was anybody looking for her? Did Arjun know?

~

'Where are you, Rupali?' Arjun was thinking aloud. He had arrived a bit late, expecting Rupali to be angry with him, but had found no one. He checked his mobile to see if there was a message. Then he called on Rupali's cellphone thinking that she might have gone back to the hostel—it was switched off.

'Come on Rupali, call me!' he said desperately and tried her number again.

~

'Shut up! Just shut up!' the guy on the front seat screamed. When Rupali didn't stop, the guy next to her held her hair in his fist and pulled her with a jerk. The impact was such that Rupali's entire body got pulled back and the back of her head collided with the other side of the van. Rupali screamed.

When, a few seconds later, she didn't stop shrieking, the guy lost his cool. He slapped her brutally. It stunned Rupali. He slapped her again. And again. And again. And again. And then again. Poor Rupali could not even bring her hands up to her face to protect herself. They were still tied behind her back.

Rupali felt her face go numb and blood spilled out of her lips. What she did not know was that her lips and her right eye were swollen. All she could feel was pain, intense pain. 'Where are you, Arjun? Why can't you find me? Please come and take me away . . .' she pleaded silently.

~

Having spent a considerable amount of time trying and failing to call Rupali on her phone, Arjun finally reached her hostel. Never before had Rupali made him wait. Not for this long. If anything, she would call him up and update him. And she would've never switched off her phone. She always kept it charged and ready in case her family called.

At her hostel, Arjun somehow managed to get hold of Saloni. He believed Saloni would know Rupali's whereabouts. But just like Arjun, Saloni too didn't have any clue.

'But she should be with you. She left the hostel about an hour and a half back,' she said.

Arjun hit his fist on his bike in frustration. He was seriously worried now. He knew how infamous the city was. A young girl—alone—walking in the dark—phone switched off, they were not good signs.

'Did she take an auto?' he asked, something suddenly striking him.

'There wasn't any auto here at that time. I stepped out along with her as I was heading towards the basketball court. Not sure if she would have taken one from the next circle. But my best guess is she won't take an auto from the next circle because from there it's walkable,' Saloni responded worriedly.

She too had called on Rupali's number several times. She directed Arjun to follow the route she knew Rupali had taken.

Something wasn't quite right, Arjun's senses told him repeatedly. He felt restless, as if something bad was going to happen, as if there was something he needed to do.

'I will follow the same road and look for her. Meanwhile, you please call up your common friends who might have any knowledge of her whereabouts. If you get any news call me.'

'Yes, I will. And if you find her, immediately call me back.'

~

The van stopped at what appeared to be an abandoned building on the outskirts of Delhi. It was a mill that had shut down many years back. Wild bushes stood tall amid the broken concrete structures. Creepers ran over the layer of foundation stones and at places clung to the walls. There was dead silence. The moonlight faintly illuminated the place. There was no other source of light. The place looked haunted.

Two of the men stepped out of the vehicle and walked around to take stock of the place, while the person next to Rupali sat holding her mouth. They were drunk, but they'd remembered to be cautious. The two who had gone for a recce came back and nodded.

The men had gone to choose a preferred corner of the mill. They zeroed in on the other side, where a renovation work was left in the middle. A partially built structure with only foundation walls rose till knee length and the pillars in the four corners rose upwards. At the top end of the columns, iron rods crept out and were left uncovered. Apart from a pile of concrete and a stack of bricks, there was heap of sand, which caught their attention. They verified that no other human was present at the site.

Rupali's heart pounded in her chest but her weak body could not support her. Her head was hurting badly. The continuous torture and the fear that something dreadful was going to happen had made her mouth go dry. She was thirsty.

The man next to her tugged at her to get her to move. The door had been opened. When Rupali tried to resist, he again caught her by her hair and pulled her along. Her feet were dragged through the uneven ground. At one point, she fell down on her knees. She cried in pain and begged the men to leave her. She fell down on their feet and requested for mercy. She reminded them of their mothers and sisters back at home. But then she was pleading to heartless men. Worse, they were drunk, as well. The man they called Babloo kicked her hand, caught her by her right arm and dragged her on. Rupali's dupatta got stuck in a bush as her body continued to get dragged away from it. She kept crying. She kept begging.

At the site, the man threw Rupali on a mountain of sand and stuffed her mouth with a thick dirty cloth. That's when her heart sank and her mind went blank with fear.

She heard them talk softly with each other. Then their leader, the one who had been directing everything, stood above Rupali. He took a big swig of alcohol while he stared at Rupali. There was a stony blankness in his eyes, as if he had no feelings. Something within Rupali died at that very moment.

Bhaiyaji pushed himself inside Rupali. Rupali's eyes split wide open in a flash. Her lifeless body throbbed for a fraction of a second. She screamed and gave voice to her unbearable agony.

Over Bhaiyaji's shoulder, Rupali stared into the moonlit quiet vast black and white sky. Perhaps, there was a God beyond that infinite sky who was looking at her in that moment. Looking at her and still doing nothing. Absolutely nothing.

And every time her body felt a thrust it burrowed further into the sand. And every time that happened, tiny gravels of sand rolled down the pile. Rupali's motionless eyes continued to look into the infinite sky, but only for a brief period after which she turned unconscious.

And then it began. It was all a blur—her clothes being torn off, the excruciating pain, the scream dying in her throat, her choking, the pain growing, the faces changing but the pain still being there—and then her fainting and regaining consciousness. Again and again and yet again. Till there was nothing left of her except a bleeding body and a vacant stare.

The sweat from their forehead fell over Rupali's eyes and her lips. Sand clung on to her hair and the sides of her body. In between her thighs, a patch of sand got soaked in blood. It was her blood. It didn't matter to the savages blinded by lust and overpowered by alcohol. They continued to tear her apart.

A beautiful innocent soul had been torn apart. The one who had always stood for the right thing had been badly wronged.

~

Arjun stood alone on the road when his phone rang. It was Saloni.

'Any news of Rupali, Arjun?' she was sobbing.

'No,' he sighed.

Behind him were his friends who had returned after searching in every possible direction. All of them had been stunned into silence.

In front of him the road stretched into the distance.

'Where are you, my love?' he sighed exasperatedly into the dark night. The silence surrounding them was dreadful.

Twenty-five

Twenty-four hours later . . .

'The patient was brought in unconscious. The initial tests have confirmed rape. Plus she had gruesome injuries. The idea was to leave her unrecognizable so she wouldn't be able to give a statement if she survived.

'She had a fractured skull and sustained severe head injuries that led to blood clotting in her brain. It appeared she had been hit on the head by either a brick or something heavy. There is also a possibility that someone smashed an alcohol bottle over her head. Looks like the men who raped her had been drinking. After raping her they tried to kill her. Under the influence of alcohol they wouldn't have been able to make out if she was dead or not. Either way, they left her to die.

'She hadn't succumbed to her injuries. But she couldn't be called alive either. The barbarity of the crime has shocked us. The patient suffered very deep cuts on her left breast and both her thighs. This led to significant blood loss from her body. But worst of all were the cuts on and around her private parts that have been disfigured beyond imagination. It appears they stabbed her more than once there.

'As part of the first surgery, several tiny pieces of glass have been pulled out of her private parts. More surgeries may be performed, but only when her condition stabilizes.

'In addition, one more round of surgery has been performed to treat her head injury. So far, the patient hasn't responded to it. Even after sixteen hours, her condition is unstable and very critical. The patient continues to be unconscious and nothing can be said unless she regains consciousness. On two occasions, for a couple of seconds, her body showed some movements in distress. Those were a result of the trauma that her brain continues to be in. Three units of blood have already been transfused and two more units are scheduled for the day.'

That's all the team of doctors had to say. After the brief from the medical team that had gathered for the press conference was over, it was the turn of the police commissioner of Delhi to update the media on the progress of the case.

'A few men from the slum near where this crime took place happened to discover the victim when they were trying to take a shortcut to their homes. Seeing her, they immediately called 100. An FIR was lodged on the very night the victim was brought to the hospital. Prima facie it's a case of rape and attempt to murder. No eyewitness has turned up so far. But the same men who called us told us about seeing a white van speeding away on the road nearby, moments before they stepped inside the dilapidated building. They said it was the only vehicle on that abandoned road and the driver was driving rashly.

'During our initial investigation, one boy talked about

having seen a white van, around the time of the girl's disappearance, suddenly stopping on the roads of North Campus and pulling a girl in. From a distance, he could not notice the vehicle number. He couldn't even confirm if that was a prank or an actual abduction. This is the same road where the victim was supposedly on as per her close friends.

'Right now, CCTV footage in and around North Campus is being scanned to trace this white van. There is a strong chance that this van is the same as the one the slum dwellers had seen. The moment the registration number of this vehicle is obtained, there won't be any delay in nabbing the perpetrators of this crime.'

The team of doctors at AIIMS and the Delhi police took some questions from the media that had gathered, after which the press conference got adjourned.

In the next few hours, the brutal and heinous gang rape of a DU girl had become breaking news in the national media. And in those stories, Rupali, who was still a living being, lost her identity.

In the medical vocabulary she became a patient.

In the terminology of law and order she became a victim.

In the language of the media, she was a rape survivor.

And unfortunately for a large part of India, she had become impure; an impurity that could not be undone by any means. A stigma was now attached, embedded in her and had become a part of her existence. Even though she had never wanted it. Even though she had resisted it. Unfortunately, she would have to live with it—if she survived. And so that the extent of her ignominy could be minimized, she was robbed of her own identity, of her real name in those media stories.

The horror of this monstrous crime caught people's attention. It shook their conscience in a way that they not only condemned it, but also wanted to do something about it. It made their blood boil in a manner that had never happened in the past. It invited outrage from across the country. It made way for a million voices that further led to an uproar across the length and breadth of the country. People questioned the law and order in the country and especially in the national capital. There were angry discussions on what the society had become. And then there were prayers for the girl who was struggling between life and death.

42 hours later . . .

The outrage against the crime continued to grow. So much so, that it spilled on to the streets. Students whose lives Rupali had been a part of—Tenzing and his music club members, Saloni and her batch of friends, Arjun's political group, and Raheema—had all come together to mobilize the crowd. They were angry and their anger took over the whole college and then the university, and then slowly consumed the city.

The scene was similar at each and every epicentre of protest. The gathering at the vast space in front of Rashtrapati Bhavan was the biggest of all, seeing which the Rapid Action Force (RAF) had been installed next to the state police. From tear gas pistols to water cannons, the law and order machinery had prepared itself to deal with the situation at hand.

A gathering of thousands at this one place was a sight to behold. Every single sound, be it the frequent voices over the hundreds of walkie-talkies in the hands of cops, the centralized loudspeaker installed over the RAF's *Vajr* van, or the news journalists reporting live, all of it added to the chaos. But the one sound that dominated and suppressed every other was the thumping hum of the crowd.

It remained undefeated.

Traffic that evening had come to a complete standstill. On a few key roads that led to the epicentres of the protest, the only vehicles allowed to enter were either the media vans or the police patrols. Everything else was in a deadlock.

Then came the moment when the much-anticipated occurrence happened.

It rained. Heavily.

Large drops that were powerful enough to disperse the crowd, to make people run away from the open streets and seek the nearest shelter, fell in sheets. The scene became even bleaker. Yet it wasn't able to break the newfound will of this nation's youth standing united for a cause. *How could a spell of rain break those who'd already prepared themselves to face the monstrous water cannons?*

Besides, they were anyway waiting for the rain . . .

60 hours later . . .

Things had changed. But not for the better. They had further deteriorated. The tests that were being conducted at regular intervals exhibited this. The numbers on the test reports, which were supposed to be closer to the normal range, were instead drifting away—some far below the minimum, some far above the maximum limits. More powerful drugs and higher doses had made their way into the arsenal of the nurses in the ICU.

The doctors didn't have much to say. So far, at different points in time, they had said the same thing in many different ways, just to make it different from what they had said before, just to make it less painful to absorb, just to keep the hopes alive. But beyond a point, you don't have much to say, especially when the test reports say it all.

The doctors had never promised the moon, but now they were not even showing the silver lining. So they resorted to their default statement.

'We are doing our best. And everything else is in the hands of God.'

No wonder the walls of hospitals hear more prayers than those of churches. But Arjun was not sure whether he was going to pin one of his own to the walls of the ICU in AIIMS. If everything was in God's hands, then what had happened to the girl he loved was also the same God's will. Why did He let that happen in the first place? What wrong had she done for which she deserved to become a feast for those monsters? Why had nobody come to save her?

Once again, the higher power had failed him.

He wasn't sure whether he should beg God to save her or hold him responsible for the events that had taken place in the past sixty hours. So he did both. That's the nature of a tragedy that threatens to take away the precious love of your life. It makes you do anything and everything, and sometimes even contradictory things.

So he abused the God in whom Rupali believed in and appealed to him as well.

Frustration and helplessness took its toll on his mind. Hunger and sleep had long escaped his life. Even though his body demanded them, his heart and mind were not at peace to look after his body. Whatever little rest he had got on the bench outside the ICU the night before made him even more restless. He had nightmares—of doctors and nurses running and trying to save Rupali. The visual of her lying unconscious on the ICU bed, with a dozen tubes piercing her body never left him in peace. It was exactly the way he had seen her, earlier in the day, when he was allowed to step inside the ICU. She was put on life support system, the doctors had told him. Machines were keeping her body alive. A thick tube that was externally connected to a ventilator ran insider her mouth, another one ran inside her right nostril, then there was one more than penetrated inside her neck. He had seen those units of saline, blood and sedatives that hung over her head. The urine bag that was tied to a corner of her bed and that white bedsheet over which showed the patches of blood that time and again was seeping out of her dressing. He had seen the monitor behind her bed that was continuously generating numerous multi-coloured graphs—he had no idea how to read them. But something in them told him that things were not well. And then there was this continuous beep generating from the monitoring machine that made this entire set-up look so delicate and critical. Those beeps continued to echo in his dreams. He wanted to run away from them. Then he heard Rupali in distress, calling out to him. He heard men around her. He wanted to save her. But for some reason, he could not make out from which direction her voice was coming. He woke up suddenly, a scream died in his throat as he saw the surroundings of the hospital.

On the one hand, he was burning from inside to avenge Rupali's misery; on the other, Rupali's critical condition was testing his endurance. Awful anger and constant fear had made their space in his heart. A combination of both was more bitter than anything he had felt before. It made his life miserable and, to add to it, time crawled and tested his patience. Even after two days, there were no answers to his questions; there was no end to his suffering.

In some moments when he couldn't digest the horrific reality of what had happened to his love, his blood boiled. He wanted to help his close friends who had joined the police in trying to hunt down the criminals, the beasts. He wanted to join his agitated party members who had called the mass protest against the system demanding justice. But every time he thought about it, he imagined his worst fears coming true. He imagined Rupali suddenly wanting him there and him not being around. And that made him step back.

'What do you mean you can't say? *Haan*? What do you mean you can't say?' Arjun shouted in anger and jumped at the doctor. 'When will she open her eyes? You are a doctor but you can't say?'

'Mr Arjun, I understand your mental condition but I'm afraid we don't have any answers at this stage . . .'

'Then who does! Who the hell does!' Arjun had lost his cool.

'Arjun! Arjun! No! No! No! Hold yourself back, Arjun!' Madhab pulled him back while he kept apologizing to the doctor on his friend's behalf.

Arjun kept asking his question in a daze, 'She is going to survive, right? You'd better tell me if she is dying.'

'Arjun, shut up! Calm down, Arjun! ARJUN!! SHUT UP!' Madhab pushed him to the wall to stop him. 'You are not going to lose it. All right? You are not going to lose it, my friend. Have some faith.'

Madhab looked into his eyes. There were tears in Arjun's eyes.

He sighed.

A ward boy arrived and stood next to them. 'You can collect the patient's clothes in room no. 204. That's the laundry room near the Emergency.'

Those were the clothes Rupali was wearing the night she was brought into the emergency ward. The cops had asked for forensic tests on them.

'You must positively claim them today, as we dispose of the patient's clothes after three days of admitting them,' the ward boy added.

Madhab nodded. He asked Arjun to have a glass of water

by the time he went and collected the clothes. Arjun wiped his tears. 'I'll go. They are Rupali's clothes. I should go.' And they hugged each other.

Then Arjun asked Madhab to check on Rupali's parents who were due to arrive any time. 'Saloni is getting them here. You take care of them, I will be back,' Arjun said while leaving to take the elevator.

In room no. 204 a heart-wrenching moment awaited Arjun. The moment he entered the room, he found himself surrounded by piles of towels, bedsheets and cushions. He walked around in a shocked state, looking for what he was there for.

That's when a housekeeping lady entered the room and, on seeing Arjun, she shouted from a distance, 'Yes mister?'

Arjun immediately reached out to her.

After taking the patient's information she took a few seconds to check her record book, after which she pointed at the extreme right corner of the room.

Arjun noticed smaller piles of clothes kept on large plastic trays. There were tags attached to each of the trays. From the bed numbers mentioned on every tag, he understood that they all belonged to various patients in the ICU. The sight of those piles of clothes, of people whom he didn't know but could empathize with, disturbed him. He sighed.

They would all have been brought in a terrible condition to the emergency ward, he thought to himself. *Did they survive? Or was he looking at dead people's clothes?* No, no, they are all alive. They will all be well, he answered to himself.

Suddenly, his eyes fell on a tag that mentioned a bed number he was familiar with. He immediately looked at the clothes and recalled how he had asked Rupali to wear that dress. The thought of Rupali wearing that salwar suit to please him made him emotional. 'She would have worn this for my sake, to make me happy,' he realized. The very dress he wanted to see her in, would have been forcefully taken off her body by those men whom he didn't know, he thought in agony. The irony made him weak on his knees.

The clothes were nearly in shreds and covered in mud and dried blood. The white churidar was soiled with dirt and now appeared cream and brown. When he stretched it in both his hands, the visual of it stabbed his chest. A pool of blood had dried at its centre as well as on both sides of the upper portion of the legs. It was Rupali's blood; his beloved's blood. He saw how it was torn off from the middle. When he tried to pick up the clothes, a dirty white sandal rolled out. He didn't find the other one.

The housekeeping lady stopped behind Arjun, 'This is all that came along with her,' she said in a soft voice.

Every inch of Rupali's clothes narrated the heart-breaking story of what had happened with her some sixty hours back. Along with them, they brought the horror of that night. They had witnessed the injustice.

Arjun grabbed all her clothes with both his hands. And that's when it fell out—a little golden heart with a small ruby on it. He picked it up. It was his gift—his confession of love!

He realized what he was holding in his hands was the aftermath of something so brutal. His girlfriend had to undergo it. Hot tears streamed down his cheeks and fell on Rupali's bloodstained clothes.

Half an hour later, when Arjun reached the ICU, Rupali's

parents and her brother had just arrived. Saloni too had walked in along with them. Madhab introduced Arjun to them.

Fate has its own destiny. Never in his weirdest dreams could Arjun have thought of meeting Rupali's parents like this. Not outside an ICU. Not holding her torn-off blood-soaked clothes stuffed in a polythene bag. Not when Rupali herself wasn't there to introduce them. What will he tell them? How shall he tell them what their daughter, who is fighting a lonely battle with death, means to him?

Saloni jumped in and said Arjun was Rupali's closest friend. Arjun bent down to touch their feet.

But those worried souls were not there to differentiate who among them was closest to their daughter. Ever since they had got the ill-fated news they had been fighting with their fears. They didn't respond. They couldn't. After a suddenly planned day and a half's journey, they wanted to see Rupali. Their tired and sleep-deprived eyes wanted to get one glimpse of their daughter. They wanted to speak to the doctors and know how exactly their daughter was doing. But before that, they had to go through the process of knowing the bitter reality.

Till then they had been kept in the dark about the real circumstances. They only knew the half-truth. Over the phone, Saloni had said that Rupali had met with an accident and that her condition was critical. She had cooked up the accident part only to lessen their shock. Back then, when she had called, the doctors hadn't confirmed anything. She hadn't even seen Rupali. It was only later that they had confirmed rape. Saloni didn't have the guts to tell them another heart-breaking news till they reached Delhi. Moreover, it wasn't going to change anything in Rupali's recovery. It would have been a terrible shock to her parents. By the time the media broke the news, Rupali's family had already boarded the train. With Rupali's identity not revealed, there was no way they could have made out that the DU girl in the newspapers was none other than their own Rupali. But the time had come when the complete truth had to be revealed.

On knowing that Rupali's family had reached, one of the doctors from the team and a senior inspector arrived at the spot. They called Rupali's parents into a closed chamber. When they saw Tanmay accompanying them, the inspector insisted that he wait outside for a while. Looking at their expressions and gauging the atmosphere, the fear on the faces of Rupali's parents began to take the worst of shapes. Meanwhile, Saloni took Tanmay along with her to the canteen. She thought she could make him eat something.

All hell broke loose the moment the truth was revealed in the closed chamber. Rupali's mother screamed out in pain. She refused to believe the fact and kept denying it.

'*Aisa nahi ho sakta . . . aisa nahi ho sakta,*' (This can't be true . . . this can't be true) she kept repeating those words in disbelief.

It took a while for the truth to sink in. Yet she kept denying it. Perhaps, in reality she wasn't actually denying it, she was denying confronting those words, the raw reality of the moment. Every subsequent time she repeated her words, the pitch of her voice kept going down. A sense of painful acceptance of the truth began emerging in every subsequent denial of hers.

'*Meri bachchi! Meri bachchi!*' (My daughter! My daughter!) came out of her mouth, after which she couldn't utter anything. Tears made their way on to the surface of the table at which she sat.

Rupali's father, who had been standing, lost his balance as soon as he heard the inspector. Arjun jumped to catch him and helped him sit on the chair behind him.

'Oh God! Oh God!' Her father wailed and held his head in his hands, cursing his ill fate. The shock of the moment didn't even let him cry. He wanted to, but something within him choked him and didn't let the pain flow out.

He let Rupali's mother weep. He didn't stop her. He didn't even look at her at that moment.

They looked completely shocked. The doctor urged them to have water, but none of them moved.

Tanmay wasn't present there to look at his parents grieving over the heartbreaking news. But then he wasn't completely unaware. He had already got a sense of the bitter reality. He had connected the dots much before he arrived at the ICU that afternoon. The front-page news of a DU girl's rape, the ICU at AIIMS, the date she was admitted, the mass protest of the college students outside the hospital where he had overheard his sister's name when someone had shouted at Saloni who was accompanying them to the hospital. He had guessed it all.

Looking at the flatscreen television installed on one of the walls of the canteen and following the breaking news of mass protest for the DU gang rape, Tanmay finally managed to politely ask Saloni, 'Is this about my sister?'

His innocent eyes didn't leave the television screen when he asked that question. He had a right to know what had happened to his sister.

He had his fingers crossed. In his heart, he desperately pleaded that Saloni would rubbish his thoughts.

But that didn't happen; not in the next moment, not in the moments after the next moment.

Saloni hugged him, tears streaming down from her eyes. So far she hadn't cried. She had been brave. But now she couldn't stop.

Tanmay could hear Saloni weeping secretly. That was his answer. He uncrossed his fingers and didn't speak a word. Later, when he met his parents again, he didn't ask them a single question. He was silent for the rest of the day. Saloni couldn't understand if that was his way to deal with the shock or if he was yet to deal with it.

Back in the closed chamber, after Saloni had arrived there with Tanmay, Arjun thought they needed to give the family some private time. The situation demanded time. He wanted to let them absorb the grave truth of the moment.

Just then Madhab came running to let Arjun know that the protests outside the hospital were getting out of control. Arjun asked Saloni to look after Rupali's family. He said he would be back soon.

72 hours later . . .

Protests had erupted in other parts of the country. People were extremely annoyed at the ever-increasing crime in society, particularly against women. And this particular incident had blown off the lid of their patience. The brutality with which Rupali had been raped and left to die had touched a raw nerve in people. They wanted stricter law and order—not just on paper, but also in action. They demanded a stringent judiciary, one that would deliver swifter justice. Status updates on Rupali's health and the progress of the case became the regular content on all media—television, newspapers and radio alike.

For all that was happening, the ruling government in the capital came under immense pressure. Delhi became highlighted as the crime capital of India. People held the government responsible for the complete lapse of law and order in the society. They wanted answers. The leaders of the party were left red-faced. Answers were demanded on every social forum. The Opposition parties saw an opportunity in the whole thing and jumped in, demanding the resignation of the leaders from the ruling party. Their motive, though, was to capture the vote bank shifting in their favour.

Under media pressure and facing the wrath of the entire country, the government was certainly placed on the back foot. The state tried to pass the buck to the Centre—because

Delhi police was controlled by the Centre, the law-and-order machinery wasn't under their control. The least it could do was to ensure that the best possible care was being provided to Rupali. With every passing hour, the story of the DU girl's rape was getting more and more of a political makeover. From the home minister to the chief minister, a series of leaders, including those from the Opposition, had paid a visit to AIIMS.

It was only late in the evening that Arjun got back to the hospital. He had thought he would be back sooner but the agitation outside the hospital premises kept him busy. He and his party were determined to keep the protests on. Meanwhile, he had paid a visit to his home to see his mother, who was equally worried about Rupali. She too wanted to visit the hospital, but Arjun suggested that she does that once Rupali regains her consciousness.

On his way back to the hospital, Arjun had got some food for Rupali's family that his mother had cooked.

Arjun asked Saloni and Madhab to leave, though Saloni insisted on staying back for some more time as Imran, her boyfriend, was supposed to pick her up. A tired Madhab assured Arjun that he was only a call away and left.

In one corner of the waiting room outside the ICU, Arjun arranged a small table and pulled up a few chairs. He placed the food and some disposable plates that he had got on the table. He then called Rupali's parents to eat.

Rupali's family, Arjun and Saloni were the only people in that special ICU ward. They were hungry, though their minds didn't register it. Caught in the most horrible day of their lives, food was the last thing on their minds. Rupali's mother resisted Arjun's invitation to eat something. The bite of bread would not go down her throat, she said. Her father wanted to see his child open her eyes and talk to him for once. Only then would he feel like eating something.

But Arjun kept insisting. Saloni joined him.

'When Rupali gains consciousness, she would not want to know that you starved. If you eat, she will get well. Please eat for her sake,' she said and gave them hope. They half-heartedly agreed and moved towards the table. Arjun and Saloni followed them as they talked between themselves.

'Any updates from the doctors?' Arjun asked Saloni.

She shook her head.

'Did he eat anything?' he asked, pointing at Tanmay.

'A sandwich at noon, when I took him to the canteen. But nothing after that. He is not talking. In the evening, when I came back from the washroom, I saw him standing at the ICU door, trying to peep through the little glass window. It's quite disturbing and painful to see him this way.'

Arjun walked up to Tanmay and gently led him to the food.

A couple of minutes later, they all sat around the table. Rupali's mother tore a bite of chapatti and poured a spoonful of curry over it. She was about to have it when all of a sudden two nurses came sprinting towards the ICU. They pushed the ICU door wide apart and rushed inside. Two surgeons came running behind them and followed them into the ICU.

The bite of chapatti fell off Rupali's mother's hand. Everyone got up from their seats. They immediately rushed to the ICU. They found the door was locked again from inside. But the family kept tapping on the door, worried about what had happened all of a sudden.

Through a small glass window, Arjun peeped inside. The curtains surrounding Rupali's bed had been pulled apart. From an angle, amid the chaos inside the ICU he happened to see her intubated face. He could see his Rupali—her face bandaged, unrecognizable.

And then he saw one of the surgeons holding two pad-like devices in his hands. He was holding on to their handles. There was panic inside. He could not hear a single word from behind the soundproof door. The surgeons and nurses plugged various devices on and off in a jiffy. A nurse was busy preparing an injection. The surgeon pressed those pads against Rupali's chest. Arjun's heart began to sink. He'd seen this only in films.

He watched in fear.

Rupali's motionless unconscious body jumped on the bed. There was no response. Another shock. Again nothing.

Arjun felt his world swim around him.

Twenty-six

Rupali took her last breath on that fateful night. They could not save her.

An innocent soul departed from the miseries of her mutilated body. Her dear ones believed so, for it made the reality minutely less difficult to bear. Perhaps, therefore, that night wasn't as fateful as the night on which the human scavengers had torn her apart. Probably, she had died that very night and for the next three nights, her unconscious body that still somehow had her heart beating inside, provided a little cushion to the shock for the people who loved her. An element of hope, no matter how small it was, that she may survive worked as that cushion.

She would never open her eyes; never speak again; never go back to her home that she had once left to pursue her education from her dream college. She would never grow old; her pictures of youth would mark the end of her journey in this world.

The worst time in any parent's life is when they have to collect the corpse of their young child and perform the last rites at the funeral. Rupali's parents belonged to that ill-fated clan of parents. Four unknown men didn't just rape their daughter. They also raped them; they raped them of their daughter. And for the rest of their lives, as long as they lived in this world, every day, when they will wake up, they will have to confront this cruel fact.

Rupali's lifeless body was cremated at a time when the city slept. The police didn't want a riot.

Her parents decided to take her ashes home, where they would immerse it in the waters of the Ganga.

A love story had been left incomplete.

She left behind a huge void in Arjun's life—a void that could never be filled. Rupali was different. She was unique in her own way. She had no match. What a loss to a life like that of Arjun's! A life that till a week back looked so promising, had suddenly been shattered. Only Arjun knew what he was going through. Unable to call her up, to listen to her voice, to touch her, he kept pulling out every tiny memory he could recall from the box of precious memories in his mind. But the more he tried to relive her memories, the more alone he felt. The more alone he felt, the more he tried to relive her memories.

It was all the more painful at night, when he was all alone, when the world slept and he tossed and turned in his bed, often crying tears that would leave the cover of his pillow wet.

It would all flash by in front of his open eyes. The little things she would say to make him feel good, her thoughts, her . . . her rationale, her stands, her wishes, her dreams . . . her dream of a DU where no Raheema would be molested again by any Mahajan . . . her dream of a society, where instead of turning a blind eye, people would come together and stand for what's right and against what's wrong . . . her dreams . . . her incomplete dreams.

Going over them again and again somewhere in his mind, Arjun had transported them all to his thoughts. In her absence, those dreams were becoming his own. It gave him some sort of solace to believe that way. It offered him a reason to live; a goal to achieve; a meaning to his life.

Left alone in the middle of an incomplete love story, Arjun took a pledge to fight for justice, for only that would bring peace to Rupali's soul. It became the larger purpose of his life.

Arjun didn't let Rupali die in people's mind. He fought with the system in her name. And he wasn't alone. He had the support of his party. He had the support of the entire university. He had the support of every Indian who had started believing that what happened with Rupali can happen to anyone and that enough was enough.

Rupali's death gave birth to a movement; a movement for change; a movement to demand stringent laws and their enforcement; a movement to call for swifter judiciary.

Three days after Rupali's death, the police had nabbed all the four accused. In his statement to the police, Bhaiyaji, the leader, admitted to raping and attempting to kill Rupali along with three of his men. He was a contract killer. He accepted that he received money from Mahajan to finish Rupali. In his statement, Bhaiyaji also confessed that he believed he had killed Rupali and that he was unsure how she had survived.

Before that day ended, Mahajan who was out on bail was booked again, this time with a non-bailable warrant in an alleged murder case registered against him. The media broke the complete news that the entire country had been waiting for.

But it didn't end there. It only marked a new beginning to a long long process of judicial trial; a trial in which the call was to treat this case as rarest of rare and demand death penalty as the only justice.

Meanwhile, Saloni had planned to move out of her hostel back to her home. She didn't want to live in that room or for that matter in that hostel any more. She wasn't prepared to live without Rupali. Before she packed her own luggage, she packed everything that belonged to Rupali. Arjun was there too, waiting outside. They would send it all to Rupali's parents.

Arjun could not stand seeing Rupali's belongings packed. They again brought back memories.

Epilogue

It is 4.00 a.m. Arjun hasn't been able to sleep the whole night, and now, he has turned on the lights in his room. He is sitting on his bed, supporting his back on a cushion. His legs are stretched out in front of him. His eyes are glued to the screen of his mobile phone.

A little smile makes its way to his lips. Unable to sleep, he is reading all the old SMSes from Rupali that are still present in his message box. Every SMS that he reads takes him back in time, when his Rupali was there with him.

The one he is reading now takes him back to the New Year's Eve when he kissed Rupali for the first time. The memories flash by in his mind. He is reliving that moment again. How her lips felt in between his! Draped by a wonderful foggy night, that intimate moment when, for the first time, he had felt a girl's body in his arms. They had shared the warmth of each other's bodies on that cold night. It was a beautiful, magical moment . . .

He looks outside his window and he can see the faint light of dawn. It's today again. The present! It's so different from the past. The past! It will never come back. Never ever! That little smile that took birth on his lips has vanished now. He scrolls down the message box. A few more moments pass.

Something makes him laugh this time. He reads the message again and then, the next moment, he looks away from his phone.

'Hell! I couldn't do it.' He is talking to himself.

And then he speaks again in the dead silence of the dawn, 'But she did it.'

He shakes his head in disbelief and, at the same time, admires the guts of the girl he loved. Again a smile makes its way to his lips.

'A first year girl proposed to a senior!' he says and thinks about it.

He continues to shake his head. The smile on his face widens and soon changes into a grin. The moment comes alive before him. His nervousness and stammering, Rupali's confident proposal . . . the planes flying above them, the noise of traffic.

He is laughing now.

'Oh Rupali!' he says, missing her even more. The pain resurfaces and he suddenly chokes on his own words. Tears rush down his eyes.

He is sobbing hard, like a kid.

'Oh Rupali . . .' he screams in pain.

He hits the bed with his hands. Again and again in frustration. She's gone . . . she's gone . . .

His eyes are red from crying. Then a thought strikes him. The noise might wake his mother up. He doesn't want her to hear him cry. He grabs the cushion behind him and tightly holds it to his chest and bites it hard. It suppresses his screams. He weeps loudly into it.

He wants to flush out all his tears in one go, so that he doesn't have to shed them again, so that he doesn't have to go through this again and again.

Slowly, he is able to regain control over himself. But he is breathless. He drops the cushion and takes a deep breath. He is calmer now.

He picks up his cellphone again. His wet eyelashes blur his vision. He scrolls down his message box. He arrives at what looks like the very first message from Rupali in his mobile phone. It dates back to the evening when they had sat on the lawns outside her hostel. It was to discuss Raheema's case. He recalls how she had said that she was scared of him since the day of the orientation. 'Did I really scare her then?' he thinks to himself.

Then suddenly, he recalls something—the plant! Rupali's tulsi plant! Something has struck his mind. He looks at the time on his mobile phone. It's 5.10 a.m. He jumps out of his bed. He rushes to the bathroom and washes his face. Suddenly, he is in a hurry. The next minute he steps out of his house and picks up something from his garage. There is more light but the sun has not risen yet.

He purposefully turns the ignition of his jeep. It disturbs the silence of the dawn. But it doesn't bother him. Arjun reverses the jeep and in no time he's on the road.

About forty-five minutes later, he is standing right next to Rupali's tulsi plant.

From a sapling only a few inches high, it has grown to well over two feet. Memories have yet again begun to play hide and seek in his mind. He recalls how, almost a year back, he had stood right at that place when he first talked to Rupali. How she had pulled this plant out of a plastic bag and shown him what she had been digging the earth for. His eyes are getting moist again. There is no way he can hold back his tears. He is tired of crying. He is embarrassed of crying yet again. But that doesn't stop the tender memories from flowing in. He recalls her face and how she had some dirt on her pretty forehead when she had rubbed her soiled hands over her face.

He kneels down and runs his hands through the leaves and the tiny flowers that have blossomed.

He realizes that he is touching a life that Rupali had once planted and nurtured. He gets a feeling that through the plant he is connecting with Rupali. He believes he is touching her—as if he is holding her in his fingers. The tiny branches slip inside the gaps of his fingers; just the way Rupali would slip her fingers within his. But he cannot see the plant very clearly any more. It's his tears that are blocking his vision again.

He recalls Rupali's words from that evening, 'This plant is a symbol of my dreams. I want to take care of it. I want to nurture it.'

He murmurs something. It seems like he is talking to the plant. '. . . Won't let your dreams die. They are mine now . . . They are mine now . . .' He repeats like a child.

He gets up and runs back to his jeep. He gets the spade he had picked up from the garage. He digs the earth around that plant and, very carefully, pulls it out from its roots along with a chunk of earth. He ties a piece of cloth around its roots.

He brings it home and plants it in his garden.

And, for the first time, he feels peace come over him, as if the young girl he loved has gently spread her pink dupatta over his face. And he smiles.

Acknowledgements

I would like to thank Vaishali Mathur, Senior Commissioning Editor, Penguin Random House, for being with me throughout my journey of writing this book—for going through the entire story, and improvising it wherever it was needed. More importantly, for ideating with me on the title that I didn't agree with in the first go. I was amazed how people loved it the day we unveiled the cover. I also want to thank my editor, Paloma Dutta, for dealing with the most difficult job of cleaning the language and fixing grammatical errors. How tiresome I find doing this part of my work! I feel blessed that someone like you is there to clean the mess that I create while writing. Last, but not the least, I want to thank my wife, Khushboo Chauhan, with whom I first brainstormed the whole plot of this story. How in our drawing room we drew the flow chart of characters along with their relationships to each other and further designed the flow of the story. But beyond everything else, I want to thank you, for not getting up early in the mornings and thereby providing me the solitude to write this book.